Harry Ni

Harry Nicholson now lives near Whitby in North Yorkshire. He grew up in Hartlepool from where his family have fished since the 16th C. He had a first career as a radio officer in the merchant navy. A second career followed in television studios.

Since retirement he has devoted himself to art, story writing, poetry, and the teaching of meditation.

*To Padmasimha
after a walk
through a rainstorm*

*Thruvasimha
2020*

By the same author:

Tom Fleck (historical novel)

Green Linnet (short stories and poems)

Wandering About (poems 1994 to 2014)

The Beveren Rabbit – breeding, showing, history, and genetics. (non-fiction)

The Black Caravel

Harry Nicholson

This first edition published 2016 by Dharmashed.

Copyright   Harry Nicholson

Cover design from an enamel by the author.

The author has asserted his moral right under the Copyright, Designs and Patent Act, 1988, to be identified as the author of this work.

All Rights reserved. Apart from any use permitted under UK copyright law no part of this publication may be reproduced, stored in a retrieval system, or transmitted, in any form or by any means without the prior written permission of the publisher, nor be otherwise circulated in any form of binding or cover other than that in which it is published and without a similar condition being imposed on the subsequent purchaser.

ISBN-13: 978-1535378086

ISBN-10: 1535378085

To the memory of Vivienne Blake,

who encouraged this story.

The Black Caravel

'Sharp as quivering hares are the Flecks. We've eyes and ears for things other folk miss.'

1

Headland

October 1536. North East England. The Durham coast.

Tom Fleck was troubled. He was troubled by images of broken ships, of arrows slicing fog. His eldest sons were involved. That inherited sense often brought pain. Today, he could do nothing and so put those pictures aside. He shook his head and rubbed the region of his heart. Three deep breaths did the trick. He tugged the pony's rope and set off again. The dog trotted in front, her black tail waving like a plume. Young Wilk led the bearded goat a few paces behind.

    Images came easy with the rhythmic stride of this high route to market. He smiled at new ideas. The headland stretched in front like a forlorn, stranded whale. Its spine lay twisted. Its blunt head reached for the sea. Cottages straggled down the face of the leviathan, like barnacled scar tissue after an incompetent harpoon thrust. There's a verse or two in that lot ... The southern belly of the great fish sloped until it sank into the stinking ooze of the Slake. The Black Slake, the same ship-holding pool of the old song, where Grendel the man-eater had slunk away to die after the giant warrior from Gotland tore off his arm . . .

The track snaked through hard dunes. Old folk recounted tales of when this was under the sea at high tide and their forebears lived safe on an island. But storms hit the coast and dumped a mile-long ridge of sand. Travellers now followed a neck of firm ground between dunes and a shallow bay to reach the town. Ewes skittered aside from the crunch of his boots as he led the loaded pony towards Hartlepool.

They paused by a litter of mossy stones where Saint Helen's chapel lay humped in decay amid the nibbled turf of Farwell Field. Higher ground now and a fine spot to rest and take in the view. This morning, crisp light threw into relief the cliffs of Whitby to the south. To the right stood Roseberry, the isolated hill that some old men called Odin's Berg. It cut the sky like a tooth above the dark moors of Cleveland.

At the faint bleat of geese he searched the sky. Necks outstretched, they streamed south, a black squall at their tails. The skein inscribed a wavering script on ragged cloud. They lost height. They'd likely rest a few days among the eelgrass at the mouth of the Tees.

He handed the pony's rope to his farm boy. 'Not far. Keep hold of her while I inspect the shrine.'

'Aye, will do.' The squint-eyed lad wiped a drip from his nose.

The pony stamped her foot. Her shaggy hair hid the white star on her forehead. He favoured black beasts that carried a white blaze; the little bitch by his heels sported the same mark. He kept for stud any creature born with such ornament.

A dozen sheep scattered on his stride to the ruin. He emptied his bladder into the lank nettles that shrouded the tumbled stones and whistled while the stingers took their nourishment. That completed, he pointed his quarterstaff. 'Wilk! Look there. Hark to the fuss. We've a visitor.'

Two towers flanked the harbour. A massive chain barrier stretched between them to seal off the port. Now the chains sank into the water to the rhythm of a work song from men who trudged around a squealing capstan. A two-masted ship, her yards lowered, crept in from the sea under the tow of four cobles.

The rowers, five to each boat, swung the vessel to starboard. Sailors took stations fore and aft and the ship nosed across the enclosed water of the Slake toward her berth. Astern of her, the tower chains ascended to chants and the squeal of iron. The old seaport of Hartlepool stood locked and safe from marauders once more.

Wilk handed him the pony rope. His boy's voice broke more each day. 'I wonder what she brings.'

'By the time we reach High Street the whole town will know. But, what a ship brings is not always a boon. Sometimes they unload a pox.' The master tousled Wilk's curls and gave back the rope. 'We've dawdled enough, bonny lad. You lead us in.'

Where the thin track met a drove-road they waited to join a procession. A line of ponies trotted past, panniers heavy with silvery mounds, guided by men from the saltpans.

These days, no armed men guarded the bastions of the north gate in the town wall. A generation had passed since the inland defences faced a threat from the Scots. Boy and man strode beneath the pointed arch and onto a stone-flagged bridleway. The paving slabs, part sunken and rutted by wheels, were dished by centuries of feet. The way led to remnants of the religious community founded by the Irish nun, Hieu, nine hundred years earlier.

They passed through cramped orchards of windstunted damsons, and between seaweed-heaped beds of strip cultivation where kale and parsnips made a show. After the distance of a few arrow shots Tom called a halt at the entrance to Grey Friary. By the friary gate the Franciscan brothers maintained a trough of sweet water for driven beasts. The pony and the goat dipped their noses and drank. From this spot a man could gaze down on the huddled thatches of fisher folk and the handsome stone houses of the new merchant class.

Below them stretched the dock where the new ship rubbed against the timbers of the quay. Shouts echoed off the town walls while labourers, bent under sacks and boxes, stacked cargo on the wharf. Activity halted and workers backed away when a tall horse clattered down the ship's ramp, a red-cloaked man in the saddle. The crowd parted, in silent awe at the rider's bravado. He spurred the horse through the arch of Middle Gate and into the town. Two helmeted foot soldiers, in green and white tunics, hurried to keep pace at the rear.

A grey-robed friar hobbled towards where Tom and Wilk rested. 'A new day, Farmer Fleck. I see you've brought our billy goat home. Did he rise to the task?'

'Aye, Friar Gilbert. Yon's a cheeky rogue, forever among the wife's cabbages. He's got all our nannies in kid and you shall take the best young'un for your fee, as agreed. I've not seen you for a good few weeks, how's the trouble?'

'Oh, an ache and a creak here and there. Shivering sickness leaves its mark, and I dread another damp winter. But this bit of sun is a gift from God.'

Tom met the faded eyes of the old man. 'You need to keep wrapped up. Wait a bit.' He freed a knot of the pony's load and peeled off two grey sheepskins. 'Here they be. The proper colour for the brethren.' He handed the skins to Friar Gilbert. 'Snuggle under these when you're abed. Keep them wool-side down to trap your body heat.'

The friar stroked the crinkled wool. 'Bless you, Thomas, and your family. I trust your household does well?'

'Our two eldest lads, Francis and Isaac, take small interest in the farm now. They've grown restless. They've gone deep sea under Ben Hood.' Tom looked away. 'They're on my mind a good deal.'

'Ah, not all sons follow their fathers. Master Hood is a staunch man, but I shall pray for them all from this day on. Your afflicted daughter, how does she fare?'

'A tragedy for a lass so bright of mind. I'd give my last strength for a cure. She keeps cheerful, though she has black days — days when I worry what's to become of her.'

'We must keep up the search. Come into the friary. Leave Wilk and his charges outside while I show you my herb garden. The plants know we're in for a hard winter and are faded back. But we'll find one to suit.'

Part sheltered from the sea breeze by waist-high walls of rounded, sea-washed boulders, the air held a memory of the lavender crop. Tom, his dog by his side, watched the old man's slender fingers pluck misty fronds of fennel and leaves of eyebright. The friar meant well, stooped amongst his beloved herbs on his stiff limbs. Ever since her pony threw the lass, he'd offered the same remedy. She'd slept with herbal pads on her eyes and quaffed the green liquor, but never knew a shaft of light. 'Brother Gilbert, should I take her to York, to a physician?'

'I don't know how to advise you. Mine's a humble medicine gleaned from local wise folk. I've no remedy for blindness from a blow to the head. A York physician would consult his Greek book, then feed leeches on her blood. He might blame a melancholy of the womb and tell you to find her a strong young husband, or some such daftness the Greeks peddled.'

Tom's eyebrows lifted. 'We've plenty of leeches in our duck pond. I could bring you some if they'd help.'

'I don't favour the draining of blood. She has my prayers. She has yours also, and a parent's prayer is more heartfelt than any friar's.' The lined face brightened. 'You might take her on pilgrimage to Becket's shrine at Canterbury. They say a touch of his blood-stained robe to the eyes can restore sight.'

'Canterbury?' He tugged at his whiskers. He'd never asked aught of the sky god, nor of his son, the nailed man. He'd known times when he'd cursed and yelled defiance into the clouds.

He stiffened at the ring of iron-shod hooves on flagstones. The red-cloaked rider from the ship approached, followed on foot by two burly men in Tudor colours. His stomach knotted at the proximity of green and white tunics. Images erupted of the day when he'd fought alongside thousands dressed the same. He gazed up into the rider's aloof eyes, but the man swept on, towards the main house. He shrugged and sent a hesitant glance toward the foot-guards.

One guard sniffed and gave a black-toothed grin. His bulky, broken-nosed companion ignored Tom but snarled at the stooped friar. With a shove of his boot against the thin backside, he pitched the old man face down into the herbs.

Tom swung his quarterstaff to block the next kick and wood thwacked on ankle. The man yelped, staggered, and lurched forwards.

'Ye bloody piss-fart! Make free with yon turd-stirrer, would ye?'

A massive fist swung at Tom's head. He ducked and the guard tottered.

'Get behind him!' The soldier yelled over his shoulder.

The skinny partner crashed through a row of comfrey to turn Tom's flank. Broken-nose made another scything sweep, but Tom swayed and the fist flew past his cheek. Hands grabbed his jerkin from behind. He back-kicked, hard. The heel of his wooden clog crunched against a shin and the attacker let go with a howl. Tom leapt sideways and spun to confront both assailants. His dog snarled and flashed her teeth.

The friar, on hands and knees amid his trampled herbs, looked up. 'This is holy ground.'

Broken-nose drew a short sword, rushed forward and thrust towards Tom's belly. He leapt backwards and whirled the quarterstaff. The blackthorn stave smashed onto the swordsman's fist. The weapon flew to one side.

While Broken-nose, knuckles in mouth, hopped a jig, and the skinny guard nursed his shin, Tom picked up the sword and flung it into a bed of nettles that smothered the friary dunghill. 'The holy man's right. This is a spot where men should keep a mild manner.'

The shadow of the cloaked man and his tall horse fell across the kneeling guard. 'So, Thwaite, yet more mischief! Stop your suck on those filthy knuckles and get up! We're hardly through the damned gate and you're in a fight.'

'This bugger is bad trouble, Sir Francis. He needs breaking.'

The rider made cold eye contact with Tom Fleck. 'How now, rustic? Who might you be that should be broken?'

Tom squared his shoulders. 'I'm a yeoman of these parts.'

'Well, yeoman of these parts, you'd best not meddle in my affairs in these parts.' He scowled at the soldiers. 'Thwaite! And you, whatever your name, you'll do naught else without my orders. Retrieve the weapon and keep close behind me.' He spurred his horse and yelled over his shoulder, 'You're hired to protect me, not brawl among cabbages, blast you!'

Friar and farmer stood together to watch the horseman head for the main door of the monastery.

Tom leaned on his staff, a rasp in his breath. 'Intelligent eyes, but a bit hard for my liking. Do you know him?'

Friar Gilbert sighed. 'This day's ship hails from Scarborough. She's brought us Cromwell's inspector, Sir Francis Bigod of the East Riding.' He lowered his voice. 'He's stamped through here before. He investigates our property, our bells, our coin, our moral behaviour. You fought at Flodden, I recall. Perhaps you met Sir John, his father, killed by the Scots that day.'

'I doubt it. I shivered with other sodden archers at the foot of that black hill. My gear would be rags alongside the shine of a knight.'

The friar rubbed his buttock. 'Sir Francis comes from worthy stock. When his father died, Cardinal Wolsey made the boy his own ward. But the grown man favours the Lutherans and is out of humour with Rome. He talks of reform. He thinks monasteries should pay for the upkeep of parish preachers. He does Cromwell's bidding. I tremble for the future.'

'Why be feared? You've but sixteen friars. You've a humble life and are a boon to the town. What's of interest to their great sort?'

Gilbert dabbed at a watery eye with the sleeve of his robe. 'Who can say? We live simply, and husband a clutch of thin acres — sweet though they be. I've feared since the king declared himself head of the church.' He lowered his voice. 'Such a blasphemy.'

'Why send an agent to our forgotten scrap of coast?'

'Proud Henry needs treasure. His eyes fix on the monasteries, for they hold a third of England's acres. He'll begin with the lesser houses, those without champions. He'll sell their land to his favourites. Bells will be smashed and the metal cast into cannon. I'm sad to have lived so long.'

Tom rested a hand on the friar's shoulder. 'Without the friary, the sick have no hospital. The town folk won't see you harmed.'

'Many are friends. But some wait to strip the lead off our roof, rotten as she is. I advise you to stay clear; only a Solomon could reckon the outcome. Hold no opinion. Bend like wheat in a gale. Powerful men will demand your longbow. Hide that weapon under childish gear in the dust of your attic. Now, go to market in peace, my son.'

With mouths agape, a small crowd pressed around the friary gate. They broke into cheers, and fists grasped

Tom's hand. Wilk stepped forward, his eyes wide. 'Him you clouted, who is he?'

'Tudor colours. I'm a fool. It's asking for trouble to knock down a king's soldier.' He tugged at his beard as he watched Friar Gilbert lead the billy goat towards a paddock. Outside the chapel door, a bulky figure in green and white glared across a hundred yards. Tom could sense the hate. He shivered. 'Let's make ourselves scarce. To market, at the trot!'

The buttressed Norman church of Saint Hilda reared above awnings, stalls, and animal pens, like a grey hen astride her mongrel brood. The square echoed to the wail of small pipes. The cobbles rang with the clatter of clogs from a circle of dancing matrons and beery fishermen. Coins chinked into clay pots. Travelling buskers enjoyed a good day.

Tom unloaded the sheepskins at the door of a warehouse and took payment. He glanced uphill, in the direction of the friary. No sign of soldiers, only two lasses who ushered a flock of raucous geese down the grassy slope. He caught Wilk's elbow and dragged him past an auction of bleating wether lambs. Against the auctioneer's bellows, he shouted into the lad's ear, 'Hunt for the freshest fish. See if there's herring. If we lose each other, I'll see you on the Fish Sands. We mustn't linger. Make sure we meet before the sun creeps through Sandwell Gate.'

He chuckled to see Wilk march off with the erect swagger of youth. He liked the young orphan. He recognised traits of himself in the lad's manner. Of years when he could boast of naught but a straight back and a pair of clogs he'd carved from a block of alder. Years when he grew into his father's old clothes. He could see his mother now, at home in the cow byre, mending those threadbare rags. Then came the day he could draw his father's illegal longbow to a man's extent.

He strolled between the stalls and bought a few items: a bag of bean seed fresh in from Holland (said to be of a climbing sort), a hank of strong twine, and four pounds of flat-cut iron nails.

'Good forenoon, Master Fleck.' Dolly Punder's round face peeped from beneath a wimple bonnet of yellowed lace.

'Ah, Dolly. Such be the crowds, I'd shambled right past your stall.' He stooped to give the old woman a hug. She returned the compliment with a whiskery kiss. 'How now, Mistress Punder? What's out of the ordinary today: fine pots from Cathay, spice from the Indies, ermine from Muscovy, Hanseatic amber from Riga?'

'Get away wi' ye. None among the fisher folk want such fancy stuff, or have coin to spare if they did.'

'You've gentry up there in the new houses. I've had invitations and can tell you the incomers like to put on a display.'

'Oh, yon lot are too fine to barter for cast-offs at my stall, though peddlers do well at their back doors. I'm happy to trade in what folk need: useful empty bottles, sewing thread, needles and pins, patching cloth, and oddments of second-hand stuff. See what I bought off a sailor. He came off the Scarborough ship.' She undid the neck of a calfskin bag and withdrew a book.

Tom stroked the leather-bound volume before he flicked through the pages. Though the text made no sense, the pen strokes seemed akin to the script in his wife's books. If the language proved to be Hebrew, Rachel's face would light up.

She squinted up. 'These old eyes never could read, but I know a rare piece when I see it. Do the squiggles speak to thee?'

'I mind none of the words. Did the sailor say how he came by the book?'

'Aye, he won it on the Baltic trade, off a Danziger, tossing dice. I gave him a canny bit of silver. He dived straight into the tavern.'

Tom opened the pouch suspended from his belt. 'Would a half-crown yield a decent margin?'

She pursed her lips, wrinkled her eyes, then held out her hand. 'Indeed so.' She flashed the slim disc of gold in the sunlight, turned the coin over to inspect the image of the double rose, checked the edges for signs of the clipper's work, nodded, and dropped it into her moneybag. 'Will you take a ball of good thread for luck?'

'I will, and thank you.' He took the gift from fingers that fought a tremble, and slipped thread and book into his leather shoulder bag.' He noted how she entwined her hands together in her lap to defeat the tremor.

Her cheeks puckered when she returned his smile, then she glanced at the sky and back to him. 'There's no word of the *Plenty* on this tide. Have you heard owt?'

'Too soon. Maybe another month before your Jack comes home.'

'I miss him. As do his wife and bairns. Deep-water ships leave women to weep. Your Rachel will miss her lads too, I dare say.'

'She does. Her mind's eye wanders far away. It's no riddle to guess where her thoughts take root.'

He met Wilk on the Fish Sands, perched on an upturned coble, telling jokes among an untidy sprawl of boys. Fisher lasses, bare-kneed and wind-burned, loitered nearby, skirts tucked into their aprons, baskets of baited lines on their heads. Their raucous laughter died away at his approach.

'Aren't your fathers in need of those lines? Them lugworms will shrivel like twigs if they're not soon in water.'

Bold blue eyes fixed on him and toothy grins erupted in bronzed faces. A squat girl broke into song: 'Master Fleck, Master Fleck, keep the worms wet, lift yer sneck.' They jigged laughing across the sand towards a row of fishing cobles on the tideline. Wilk sputtered, hand over mouth.

Tom took hold of Wilk's ear. 'Have a care. Don't smirk so much. That lot will be casting bride eyes at you afore too long. Now, what about fish?'

'Jonty Punder's put some aside, sir. His coble's in the lee of the groyne, yonder. The pony's tethered alongside.'

Still gripping Wilk's ear he led him to the coble. They squeezed between a dozen tar-bottomed boats hauled out on the sand, to where a fisherman worked on a suspended net. In the brown fingers, a hand shuttle weaved thread backwards and forwards across a rent. Tom released Wilk's ear and scanned the town wall. The old ramparts showed a scatter of women who gossiped as they draped washed clothes along the yellow stones. He relaxed.

'Well met, John. You've a few fish for me?'

Bronzed wrinkles surrounded grey eyes. 'Now then, Master Fleck. Mebbe I have.' He put down the shuttle. 'Of late, the nets fill enough to crick a man's back.'

Tom leaned against the clinker-built hull. 'Take care of that back. A man's brawn keeps his belly full.'

'True enough. Jack's my eldest. I hope he's home afore too long, I could do with his muscle.' He scratched his full beard with broken and fish-scaled fingernails. A smattering of scales remained suspended in his whiskers. 'And there's nay word of the *Plenty*.'

'I want them home too. But, what's in the landings? My Rachel's kitchen needs fish to pickle.'

'I've a score of fat herring and a bold cod that might serve.' He pulled back a piece of threadbare canvas to reveal a pile of fish gleaming on a bed of seaweed. 'These swam happy and gay at daybreak. Will they do?'

'Handsome fish. Same price as last week?'

'Aye, fourpence. No need for extra while they're close inshore.'

Tom counted out small silver onto the fisherman's cracked palm. He took the fish and packed them, bedded on seaweed, into the pony's baskets.

'Thank you. Will you take this fat fellow for luck?' John dipped into a wooden bucket and pulled out a dripping, red-brown crab. The pointed tips of its legs groped in vain for a surface, while its great claws lifted in defiance despite twine that bound them tight.

'Thank you. But, handsome though he be, my wife won't boil him.'

'Ah, maybe she's heard that crabs feed off drowned sailors. Some folk won't touch them for fear it's true.'

'Aye, a mislike of some sort. Well, I must away now. She's doing a big dinner. You keep safe on the sea, old friend.'

'And Mary walk by your side, Master Fleck.'

They led the pony out through the town gate.

'Master, I reckon crabs taste grand. Why won't Mistress cook them?

'Did you see his terrible claws? Perhaps such a one frightened her when a child. Now, you take the quick track home and set out the fish on the dairy cold slab. Scatter parsley on top to keep the flies off. I'll not be long behind. I'll walk by the dunes and check on the heifers at North Warren.'

'Aye, master. I'll not dawdle. I'm famished.' The boy set off at a jog with the pony in tow.

2

The Black-haired One

Crimdon Hall on the Durham Coast, the same day.

Rachel Fleck read the letter once more. The packet came from a London lawyer. It settled a question of late on her mind: how fared Alvaro? There'd been no word for a year, and now this. The lawyer wrote how his client, Alvaro Jurnet, named her in his will and bequeathed her five-hundred of King Henry's gold sovereigns. Also, Master Jurnet sent her a message, a letter folded within the will a dozen years:

Dear Rachel, daughter of my lifelong friend, Isaac Coronel, if I own wealth at the end of life, I gift you a portion. I leave you with this thought: the world is but shadow cast upon the walls of a cave by the fires of men. Stay true to our people. Be without fear — fear is but shadow.
'L'Chaim!'
Alvaro.

Her long fingers folded the parchment. Thought ceased for a moment while she fitted the broken halves of the wax seal together to leave a hairline crack. She blinked away tears and faced the window with unfocussed eyes. The old days come to an end, and Alvaro bids farewell with the words of Plato. I hope he knew peace and did not suffer. I hope he sits at ease now, in discourse on learned matters with my father, sipping wine in the shade of an olive grove, Solomon's Temple bright across the valley. But, Father knew the *Book of Zohar.* He claimed we take a new birth. So, where are they now?

Beyond the lead-lattice windowpanes, her blurred gaze rested on the pear tree. The trained espalier hung against the red-brick garden wall like the Christians' image of their tortured saviour, stretched and nailed. Horizontal branches, and the few late-clinging leaves, jolted into focus. Through the rattle of pans and the laughter of servants from the kitchen, the clatter of a horse echoed around the cobbled yard. At the tread of heavy boots she rose and unlatched the door. The broad form of a florid-faced priest advanced towards her. His black, ankle-length cassock showed saddle creases.

'Mistress Fleck? I'm Master Burgoyne, Vicar of Hart. Good forenoon to you. A fine day — this wind aside.'

'Good forenoon, Master Burgoyne. Please come in. May I offer refreshment?'

'Thank you, but I won't enter, though the smells from your kitchen tempt the senses. I've already imbibed enough today; I'm new here and everyone wants me to take ale and cake.' He gazed upwards, at the regular courses of yellow and grey stone and at the crisp, chisel-cut window lintels. 'This puts my time-worn church and residence to shame. You are fortunate to dwell in such a handsome and modern structure. I'd heard Thomas Fleck is but a yeoman farmer.'

'Such he declares himself.'

'Then he's a modest but successful man and I'd like to meet him. Today, I've come about his children.'

'Our children? Which of them? Two are already fine young men.'

'Indeed, I'm told the Good Lord has blessed this house with health and fertility for twenty years. However, I'm your priest and I'm troubled to hear whispers of negligence of baptism. Also, in my first month in this parish, I've yet to welcome any from this house through my church door.'

'We attend the marriages and burials of friends, and the baptisms of their children.'

'But never the baptisms of your own. Aren't you concerned for your children's souls? Man is born in sin and can enter heaven only through baptism.'

Rachel stood equal to his height and returned his glare with a cool gaze until the priest's blood-flecked eyes glanced away. She measured out her words as though she picked them from a purse: 'My husband attends the market. His way home comes through those of our fields that fringe the dunes.'

He frowned. 'Then I'll call on my return journey. Good day to you, Mistress Fleck.'

'And good day to you, Master Burgoyne.' She closed the door, then guided its iron sneck home. She rested her forehead against the door's oaken frame where she murmured in Hebrew until her breath grew regular and her heart relaxed. A minute passed before she straightened at the footsteps of her two youngest, who scampered from the kitchen.

'Mam, see what cook's made for me and David.' Rebecca held out a biscuit in the shape of a man with splayed arms and legs.

'Oh, what a perfect biscuit-man. But don't eat him now, lest he spoil your meal.' She pushed aside a lock of her daughter's red hair and smiled into the angular, freckled face.

'She's already bit the head off mine.' The round-faced brother broke into a sob.

'Did you bite the head off little David's man? Be careful to speak the truth.'

Rebecca shuffled her feet. 'Only because he nipped me.'

'David, you nipped your sister? A cruel trick. Why do that?'

'She said I'm fat.'

'He said I'm skinny.'

'That will do. I've heard enough. I know you love each other, therefore I will ask for Solomon's judgment of the matter.' She faced upwards, into the adzed beams of the farmhouse. 'Oh, wise King Solomon, we implore thee, help us with your wisdom. What shall we do with these children and the biscuit-men?'

She held out her hands, palms upwards, and closed her eyes. The children held their breath until she rested a palm on each head of curls. 'King Solomon says to sit in the garden, smell the last few flowers in the lavender bed and count the butterfly people who drink there. Don't harm them. Take care to count the red ones, then count the white and see which is the greater. Stay hushed and listen for the return of Kate and your father. I sense them coming. Give me the biscuit-men while you obey.'

On the track home, wind laden with fine sand hit Tom Fleck's face on the summit of the mound. The long pile persisted — an island of rock and clay anchored in waves of silver dunes that inched inland to smother his pastures. Ah well, he owned fields enough. Years ago, in threadbare rags, he'd have taken a mattock and, in the hunt for treasure, cut a slot through this burial place. But, no bother, let the old ones rest. These days he'd no need to steal their crumpled ornaments to buy his bread. The sleepers lay beneath his own turf. Folk from the deep past; their names forgotten, but he sensed them as if he shared their blood. Words surfaced. The start of a verse: *Time lays a green cloak across the mound. The laughter and the whimperings now tiny whispers beneath the feet.*

To the south, the heather hills of Cleveland stretched east and west. On those hills he'd helped his father cut a trench into a mound such as this. They'd trenched dozens of them over the years for trinkets to sell to the traveller Jew. Dad's forebears gave him a rare nose for mound digging. The man's mattock kept the family from starvation. The pittance earned labouring for the Manor would never satisfy a stomach.

One day, shrouded in fog, and thirty miles to the south, a trench through such a decayed hummock uncovered the way to Rachel. He'd tramped to Northallerton bearing the gold necklet of some ancient chief. Her father, Isaac Coronel, forgot his dealer's customary stone face and gasped aloud when he uncoiled the length of woven gold. 'Look here and here,' the Jewish dealer exclaimed. He'd pointed a trembling finger at the ends of the rope. 'See these delicate dragon heads? Such exquisite workmanship! You bring an object more rare than aught your father ever offered.' In one swift movement, Isaac formed the rope of gold into a circle and, with a flourish, draped it around Rachel's neck. 'Behold! My daughter becomes a Brigantian princess! Witness how the ancient craftsman's passion lives again.'

With a light step and eighteen gold sovereigns he'd rushed home from Northallerton to his ill sister in the broken-down cow byre. Months slipped by. Flodden came, and he survived. The next time he'd set eyes on the chieftain's gold it gleamed in the sun at Rachel's throat on the day she became his wife. They'd handfasted beneath trees in Northumberland, at the side of her father's grave.

One swipe of his clog spread a molehill. In the fan of sandy soil a dull eye stared back – a fragment of red earthenware. The dog sniffed the shard. 'Nowt there to sweeten thy tooth, Nell. Any meat yon pot held is long gone.' His work-hardened fingers fondled the dog's ears. She responded with the kiss of a cold nose and a lick.

He crouched at the base of the salt-shrivelled hawthorn that crowned the squat summit. It gave a bit of shelter. Overhead, a raven croaked in its clumsy squabble with a fork-tailed kite. At each thrust of the black beak, the kite flipped and slid through the air with a derisory mew.

The tide hung full. Close inshore, the ocean lay in a state of rest. His longbow could drop a clothyard arrow into yon calm patch where the water glittered. Yet, over a mile out, on the cold green chop, deep-laden ships heeled over and beat south. Bleached sails heaved in sunlight against columns of black cloud that built before his eyes. Those dark pillars seemed determined to grasp and pull down heaven.

Inshore, five men in a coble heaved on lines. In haste, they unhooked fish and cast them into baskets. Their keen eyes knew the weather. Would those towering squalls find his two sons? A fortnight since, he'd lingered on the headland until their ship vanished beneath the rim of the sky. He hoped they had moored safe on the Flanders shore.

Nell raced two wide circles around him and the tree, then darted with one bark into the dunes. She'd found Kate, his fourth child, the black-haired one. She'd be nestled out of the wind, in a hollow of the sand hills, in her favourite spot among the burnet roses. Seventeen and sharing her mind among the birds. The sightless lass who sees more than most.

The middling weight, the press of warm toes, and the bite of delicate nails on her wrist, told of a thrush. Her palm sensed the warm breast of the bird who picked at the cake crumbs. A whirr passed by her face and a breeze touched her eyes. Some sprite landed on her wimple bonnet before fluttering to her shoulder. The new bird fidgeted. Tiny claws tangled for a moment in her woollens. Bold cock robin, impatient for his turn.

A tickle and a kiss of air fluttered around her ankles. It would be those cheeky chaffinches that sighted folk called 'seven-coloured linnets.' She brought to mind the plump little bird and tried to visualise his colours one at a time. She pictured the pink breast and cheeks, the blue cap, the black and white wing bars, the brown back ... The wrinkle-faced mastiff, asleep at her side, flicked his tail and her palm lifted. The thrush fled. The finches scattered.

She listened to the breeze, the croak of the raven, the mew of the kite. A patch of sun settled to bathe her face and heat the dune. She touched the top layer. Silken sand trickled warm through her fingers. Her strong, spinner's hands pushed deeper, through the knotted roots of the marram grass, to meet a chill. One by one, the birds returned. She extended a hand for the thrush. The plump form settled on her wrist.

She spoke to it with thought, 'Hello again, you who sing your notes twice.' She reached out with her mind again, 'And you too, Father. I know you watch. You're soon back from market. Come down from the mound and tell me all the news.' She listened to him stride through the sand-hill roses, listened to the scrape of burnet thorns on his leather-clad legs. Nell had already plunged down the slope, licked her cheek, and now danced around her mastiff.

Tom sat at her side and took her hand. 'Friar Gilbert sends you his best fresh herbs. A ship has docked from Scarborough. And I bought a rare book from Dolly Punder.'

'A rare book? Read me a page, please.'

'It's in foreign, so I can't. The script has a Hebrew look. We'll see what your mam reckons.'

'Exciting! What did you see from the hillock?'

'Two ships far out, and a coble close in. Now, we can't sit long, your mother lays out the feast. You know this day is special for her.'

She held up an empty snail shell. He noticed, around her wrist, a braided band of marram grass; another rested around the neck of the mastiff — bright green on a smooth coat of brown.

'First, tell me of this shell. It has ridges.'

'Yellow and brown stripes. It's of the banded tribe who live amid the dunes.'

'I remember them, they're pretty.' She passed him a small, egg-shaped lump. 'Feel how smooth.'

Tom let the pebble gleam in the sunlight. 'It's a bonny bit of amber. A clear glow and a tiny fly trapped inside. A special jewel. Did you find it on the shore?'

'Wilk gave it me, yesterday. He found it in a rock pool and gave it a polish. He'll drill a hole and thread a cord for me to wear.'

'Wilk makes you little gifts?'

'A few. He's gentle natured, but I've asked him not to peep. I can sense the touch of eyes.'

Tom grunted, picked up a round pebble and hurled it across the dunes. His dog, Nell, set off in pursuit. 'I'll speak to him.'

She reached out and grabbed at his tunic. 'No, please don't. Wilk means no harm, he's a sweet boy.'

Tom took her by the shoulders and they stood together. 'So he is, my lass. But mebbe a bit too sweet on you.'

Father and daughter faced the sea for a while and listened to the breeze whisper through the dune grasses. A squeal broke their thoughts. Nell padded up — a rabbit in her jaws. Tom Fleck fondled the mongrel's ears. 'Well done. Be sure to take it home to the kitchen. Off you trot.' He turned to Kate. 'Don't fret, love. There'll be no nest of young left to starve. He's a buck. Now take my arm, we don't want them fierce burnets to snag your frock.'

'There's no need. Bull knows to skirt round thorns and cowpats.'

'Aye, but he stops everywhere to sniff, and we lack time for that.'

'Well then, I'll link you this day of remembrance of Grandfather Isaac.'

'Good. He'd approve of you. He also knew the joy of a quiet mind.'

Father and daughter strolled along the sand track. The marram grass whispered against their legs and sprang back in blue arcs.

'Mam says her dad loved you.'

'And I him. I still feel his presence. A shame you never knew the man.'

She sensed his gaze and knew he looked her over. 'My ears tell me I've grown taller than you, Father.'

He pondered the fact that his children had not known his hunger. 'Aye, perhaps. Not by much though. There's still a barley grain between us. You've become like your mam.'

'Have I? And how might that be?'

'Oh, nowt. Take no notice.' With a hiss of papery wings a green dragonfly swished past. 'There goes the devil's darning needle. A bit late in the year for him.'

'Dad, I'd like to know why you think I've become like Mam. Eight years are gone by since our eyes met. I've a mere child's image of her — but my fingers say she's still lovely.'

He paused to untangle a briar that snagged his stocking. 'Here's a thorny bit. The track's overgrown. I'll squeeze through first and you hold my hand.'

'You see why it's easier to follow Bull's rope? He doesn't care for burnet spines either. Now, say why I'm like my mother.'

'Well, you knew I crouched atop yon mound. How did you know?'

'Ah, a tremor between my eyes. Then a picture in my heart of you beneath the thorn tree.'

'And your call fluttered inside me. 'Come down off the mound,' you said. So, now you know. You're another heart-toucher. You've swallowed the moon, same as her. Don't forget though, the gift runs in my family too. Make the most of it while it's there. If you take after me it will fade with the years. The flame passes on. Meanwhile, best keep such matters to yourself.'

'I know enough to take care. And what else do I share with Mother?' She heard him breathe out slow.

'Ah, now then. Hair the colour of fresh broken coal. Oval face. Skin, the glow of honey. Grace of swan on water …'

'Oh, now I feel a blush. Am I different in some ways?'

'Aye, girl, your eyes be light. They're blue like mine, but with the violet cast of my mother's. Careful here, for there's a bold ruffian of a woolly-leafed thistle.' He put his boot on the plant and pressed it flat.

'I know him, he's stabbed me before. But his seed heads caress like the softest silk. Has the blossom gone?'

'Long since. Back in July he flaunted a ruby topknot, a bit like the great stone on the ring of the bishop. The spear thistle wields a short lance, though. His spines cannot cut a man so deep.'

'Meaning the bishop cuts men deep?'

He coughed. 'No, I spoke wrong there. He can't do that, according to the rules.'

'There are rules on how to cut men?' She heard him sigh.

'Church rules. While a bishop will stand in line with the king's army, it's deemed unfit for his holy rank to cut men's flesh. Instead, he's granted leave to set about him with a mace and brain his fellow man. The bishops did some head bashing on Flodden Field. From here, the way broadens. Take my arm.' Her touch quivered. 'Sorry, lass, I shouldn't speak of such times. I try not to backwards cast my mind, but memory can pounce like fox on rabbit.'

'I know. I've heard you call out at night. And I've sometimes helped Mam hold you and tell you it's but a dream.'

He stopped and faced her. 'Have you now? Well, I'll only say the pictures fade over time. Do my bad nights frighten you?'

'Not frighten, though I quake to hear of such wounds. You've seen folk die at the will of kings. We should not forget them.'

His eye watered. He wiped it. 'You bring me comfort.'

She wrapped her fingers around his. 'If you need to speak, my ear is yours. And I crave knowledge of the world beyond Crimdon Hall. You could talk of the places you've seen and what you've learned. It will help my tales. I fashion stories in pictures on soft parchment and score them deep with an iron nail. I can trace the outline later with a fingertip. A sort of writing.' They set off again, across older dunes where young willow and buckthorn promised woodland to come.

'A brave idea. Francis and Isaac will fetch you a sea-chest of tales when they return.'

'Yes, and they've promised cambric cloth from Flanders. I'll make you a shirt. But my parchment pictures . . . I could make grooves to serve for letters if someone taught me how to write.'

'I doubt if parchment would hold such marks for long.'

'Then the twins will write for me in ink. I'll recite to them from memory. You shall be the storyteller and I'll be your scribe. We'll set down your poems.'

He squeezed her hand. 'I like the idea. And all the more if your own poems be yoked to mine. You cannot hold verse in your head forever.'

She returned the squeeze. 'Such a book we will make. Our rhymes and stories together ...'

'Mind these yards of poached ground where the heifers gather. We'll pick our way round the clarts. You'd not need much costly parchment for my words, I've known but one adventure. Now those ships out there, those two that beat south from the Tyne, their hulls could speak tales. I've a friend on the salt sea. We met after he deserted a cruel ship. Later, we hid together, through a long night, under a churchyard yew after the bitter rain of Flodden and ten-thousand dead. Sorry! I blather on.'

'Do you sometimes meet your friend?'

'Here's the steep bit, up and over the last dune, go canny. Peter Tindall's a merchant now. Has his own ship. On a good day our paths might cross at market.'

'Is Peter head of a family?'

'Aye, and lives content. Though he'd not a farthing to scratch his backside on, he came away from Flodden, gold heavy. One of those mace-swinging bishops gave him a bag of Scotch coin in exchange for his life.'

'A good story. He began anew. I'd like to start again, but keep my sight . . . ' She faltered.

'A loss, Kate, but you've gained other skills. There's your spinning and the tapestries you raise by touch alone, pictures so lovely that folk are loath to hang them on the wall lest the moths chew them. You walk a world of beauty.' He stopped and hugged her. 'And you're the best milkmaid a yeoman could wish for. The beasts don't fret when they know your touch.'

'I lullaby them and they let down their milk. The cows like to hear the milking ballads I learnt from you.' She giggled and broke off to sing:

'I cannot get to my love
his freckles to see
for the flood o' the Tees
runs between him and me.

I must wait on the moon
when the heron gans yem,
and the shiv'ring salmon
has done her last run.

When the watter o' the wath
drains down to the sea,
then I'll sharp gan across
and I'll sit on his knee.

We'll sing the words fluted
since Adam was born,
like the coo o' the cushat
from yonder blackthorn.'

'You've a voice like a new day, Kate. Clear enough to shame a merle.'

Tom paused at the sight of his children in the garden, counting the butterflies. They smiled as they knelt to sniff the lavender, then peep at each other and giggle. His deep voice swept across the yard, 'What be you pair of jackdaws up to?'

'King Solomon has judged us,' David squeaked. 'We must count the butterfly people until the biscuit man gets his head back.'

'Here are the men, complete with heads.' Rachel, in the doorway, held out her hands, a biscuit in each. 'For the sake of peace in this world, you may eat them now. Be sure to keep clean, we've important folk coming.' The children took the biscuits and skipped off to the barn.

Tom put his lips close to Kate's ear. 'Some days I think this household has fair gone mad.'

3

To Life

Crimdon Hall, at the close of Market Day:

With kindred at his side, Tom Fleck glanced down the long oak table that dominated the great room of his farmhouse. Whiskered farmers and their wives crowded the far end. Tonight, at ease with family and solid, farming neighbours, he could be content. The room hung with vapours from jugs of mulled elderberry wine, mild ale and strong beer, from dishes of baked onions and mashed turnip, from dismembered roast goose and carved hot beef in gravy. The two plump servant girls, sisters both, faces aglow, leaned across shoulders to clear away bowls and trenchers. He met his friend's eye and nodded. The flagstones squealed as Captain Jackson pushed back his massive chair and stood, spear-straight. Along the table, hands smooth and hands gnarled raised wine goblets and ale tankards in salute.

'Another year ripens, and ripens well,' announced the captain. His words resonated deep in his Northumbrian throat. 'We enjoyed a ploughman's winter, hard with pest-killing frost in proper time, each freeze followed by thaw, just as we like it. The spring acres waved with young barley. Bees droned long in orchards. A gentle harvest time kissed us like a maid, and now our barns quake under the weight of it all. We can be content.'

'More content than some that dwell in Tudor London and have to keep their heads down,' croaked an elderly voice. 'More content than poor Anne Boleyn what's got no head — '

A fleshy hand slapped on knotted brown fingers. 'Shush, husband, you've quaffed far too much. With talk like that you'll lose your own turnip!'

'Give over, woman! My head's nay turnip! I descend from chiefs of the Northmen. Show respect. And I'm old enough to remember Richard of York. Didn't I stand at Bosworth alongside him on that black day? My true king! There'll be no other!'

The captain stifled a chuckle and rapped the table with the bone handle of his knife. 'You're a staunch man, William, and you did your best. The times are still troubled, but for tonight let's hear no more of Southern matters. Tonight we are a gathering of good hearts. Thomas and Rachel settled at Crimdon Hall more than twenty years ago. Each year since then, on this day, they invite us to gather, share friendship, and celebrate the memory of Rachel's father, Isaac Coronel. We mark his life. We honour his wisdom,' he glanced at Tom, 'and his inspiration. Most here did not meet him, for he sleeps in a quiet wood in Northumberland, but all good folk will toast an honourable man. To Isaac Coronel. Let his virtues live!' He raised his goblet.

Chair legs scraped and the feasters stood. 'Isaac Coronel!' The light lilts of women mingled with the rounded and slow vowels of men.

Before their lips touched wine, Rachel and Tom followed with the most ancient of Hebrew toasts, in muted voices: 'L'Chaim!' Captain Edward Jackson glanced their way and responded, 'To life!'

Tankards and goblets thudded onto the table. Soft lips and whiskered mouths were wiped. Discrete burps were made. The chatter and laughter swelled above a clatter of hooves in the yard, but Tom shot a glance at his wife.

A servant girl lowered her head between him and Rachel. 'The new vicar's here. He's making fast his horse. What shall I say?'

'I'll deal with him.' Tom stood.

Rachel grasped his hand. 'Be careful. Remember to breathe slow and even.' She glanced at the rugged man seated opposite and made a quick appeal with her eyes.

Captain Jackson nodded. 'Tom and I will speak with him in another room. Aye, and a bottle of old claret shall ease the matter.'

'Welcome to Crimdon Hall, Master Burgoyne. I'm Thomas Fleck. I farm the acres along the coast from Crimdon Dene to Low Throston, and inland to High Warren and down to the Slake. By my side is Captain Edward Jackson.' Tom offered his hand to the vicar.

The vicar grasped Jackson's hand instead. 'I know Edward; we meet each Sunday at my church. I've not met you before today, Farmer Fleck. I've not seen you at church.' He settled in the most comfortable armchair and scanned the tapestries and oil paintings. 'Those make fine decorations. I'm surprised to meet such in a Durham yeoman's house.'

'Aye, some be my daughter's work. Others knew a life in London, and before then they draped Portuguese walls. Will you take wine?' Tom held up a long-necked bottle and prepared to fill three goblets.

'I will. Thank you.' Burgoyne's gaze settled on the stream of ruby liquid. 'I've come to discuss matters of baptism.'

Edward Jackson lifted a goblet, eased his wide shoulders into the armchair, and stretched out his long legs. 'Are you settled in your new parish, Vicar?'

'The speech of the local labourers grates on my ear, but I hope for better times; though I am daunted when I hear of the east winds from Muscovy; how they blast this coast in winter.'

Tom noted the priest's flaccid cheeks and their network of broken veins, marks of a poor constitution or those of a copious drinker. 'In time, your blood will thicken.' He sipped at his wine and stared at Burgoyne through narrowed lids. He recalled another priest, long ago in Alnwick, the sort inclined to burn a man.

The vicar contrived a thin smile and drank deep. 'Let's hope, for I'm often chilled to the marrow.'

Tom refreshed Burgoyne's drink, 'I was out when you called, this forenoon. On my way back from market I checked the pastured ewes. And some black heifers that roam the harder dunes — they're young female kine I favour as breeding stock.'

Burgoyne quaffed a mouthful of claret. 'I'm fully aware of such husbandry terms. My last parish nestled in the fat cattle lands of Herefordshire yeomen.' He wiped his lips. 'In the fertile valley of the Wye, men breed beasts to dwarf those of this windswept shore.'

Tom banged the table and leaned forward. 'You reckon? Then I'll send a man to Hereford town to buy me her shire's best bull. Though mebbe not. I've a black colossus in the barn who would toss the Hereford like a dog. I call him Satan.' The words tumbled out before he could halt them. He missed the affable and broad-minded previous vicar of Hart; he would be wary of the new man.

Captain Jackson slapped the arm of his chair, 'No doubt each shire rears her giants. England's kine come in a multitude of colours and form. Such diversity in cattle and people keeps our country virile and the envy of those beyond Calais, wouldn't you say, Vicar?'

'Most certainly. We are most fortunate, indeed. The bowmen of the Welsh Marches and the billmen of the north country make England's walls, as the French and Scots understand right well.'

Tom's eyes narrowed once more. 'You've known battle?'

Again Jackson broke in: 'I commanded archers. I captained Tom at the skirmish on Milfield Plain and at the great battle of Flodden Field. There's no finer bowman. Twice he kept me from death. I owe the man my life. Like mist, twenty-three years sweep away. We've become brothers.' He raised his drink.

The priest gulped his wine and coughed. 'Farmer Fleck is a sound man to keep at one's side.'

The captain recharged the priest's drink and his own, but ignored Tom's half-empty vessel.

Tom noticed and gave a slight nod. He met Burgoyne's gaze. 'You may use my given name. As for my worth, I do what any man might do for a fellow mortal.'

'And I do bear the message of The Saviour to the people of this parish, Thomas. I trust you will attend a sermon or two of mine, once you've attended to your heavy cattle, that is. My goodness, but you serve superior claret; unusual to find such in the northern waste.'

The captain smiled. 'Waste no longer. We've had five-hundred years to recover from William of Normandy's punishment. We fought for our freedom and paid a terrible price thereby. This is the country blessed by Columba, Hilda, Oswald, and Bede.'

'Ah, you know your saints, Edward, but you overlook Wilfred. The woman, Hilda of Whitby, hosted the great Wilfred of Ripon at her abbey in the Year of Our Lord 664. His presence at the Synod decided matters in The Holy Father's favour. Wilfred brought the grace of Rome to these wayward parts. It's Wilfred's gift that we celebrate Easter at the proper time and not the date favoured by the itinerant Irish Celt.' The priest's gaze drifted towards Tom's writing desk and his collection of books. 'I'm relaxed here. In this house, a scholar might exercise his mind. Few men in these parts have faculty for learned debate. I feared I'd succumb to stiffness of the brain on this coast. Therefore, Thomas, I hope I may call again.'

Tom leaned back in his chair. 'In my youth, two rare but different men, and one woman, helped lift my mind from the bog of ignorance. The older I grow, the more I thank them. My door stands open to their kind. Open to folk who hold light opinion and cherish tolerance.' He rose and gazed down on the priest. 'Come join the table. You will know some of our friends.'

'Gracious of you. I've supped a deal of your fine claret, and this forenoon the faithful plied me with ale at each house. Time to lay solid food on top. Edward, give me your hand and help me from this chair.'

Loud talk and laughter faded when the three men entered the firelight of the room. Tom exchanged a glance with Rachel as the captain guided Master Burgoyne to a spare seat. The priest settled his fleshy body into a padded chair opposite Hilda Jackson, the captain's slender, red-haired wife.

The priest beamed and folded his palms. 'Good afternoon to you all. I regret I'm late for the party, but pray continue the jollity, I'm in need of a little mirth.'

After Rachel completed the introductions the priest's attention slid to the girl at his side. 'Such a stream of new names for this weary head. I've mislaid yours already.' Kate's fingers wavered towards a dish of cakes. He contemplated her and understood. 'Let me help you.'

'My name is Katherine Fleck, and thank you — but I manage.' She chose one of her own queen cakes.

'You are Thomas Fleck's daughter? A pretty member of a fecund family. Are you the first born of several?'

She sensed his tentacled mind and shrank away, but recovered and sat erect. 'There were eight of us, but death took one. My brothers, Francis and Isaac, are eldest. They've shipped to Flanders as crew of the *Plenty*. The twins are fifteen and, now they've escaped table, are out on their ponies. The uproar in the garden comes from the smallest two.' She responded to the unspoken question, 'I'm seventeen and lost my sight at ten.'

Hilda leaned between them, 'Roast beef, Vicar? We've beans and kale to set alongside. Here's new bread and a clean trencher.'

'Ah, Mistress Jackson, I will partake. Your captain husband was most considerate to escort me to the table. I've enjoyed fine conversation with him.'

'And with my brother too, no doubt?'

'Your brother, mistress?'

'Yes. Tom is my brother.'

'Ah! Now I understand why the captain claimed brotherhood with Thomas.'

'Not so, Vicar. Their brotherhood is a bond more profound than a marriage contract.'

'Indeed?' The priest's eyes lost focus for a moment.

A fair man, of apple cheeks, reached for a water bowl to rinse his fingers and thumb. He spoke a light voice, 'I'm Ralph Warren. I wonder if you took holy orders at Cambridge.'

'I did attend that noble seminary.'

'Would that be in the days of the great Erasmus?'

'I attended his lectures.' The priest did his best to stifle a burp. 'A man of peculiar and modern opinion. Are you acquainted of his ideas, sir?'

'Thoroughly. I find Erasmus a stimulant to the mind, and he gives the Pope some exercise. I read all I find of him.'

The priest wiped the edge of his overflowed trencher board with a lump of bread and sucked out the gravy.

'We must live in accord with change. The Pope is no longer head of England's church since King Henry assumed the supreme office two years ago. Erasmus, at least, has attempted to caution the heretic Luther.'

'The monarch favours the mind of Erasmus, they exchange letters. Our own Bishop Tunstall is also a friend of Erasmus and has the king's regard —'

Tom broke in, 'I interrupt you, Ralph, but I want to say that Brian Tunstall, the bishop's brother, died on our right flank at Flodden. And, more importantly, Durham has a rare and good bishop in Cuthbert Tunstall. He's a man reluctant to burn heretics ... '

Ralph gave Tom a glance that warned, and took back the conversation. 'Yes, our Lord Bishop is both studious and gentle, like his namesake saint. For my part, I teach the offspring of merchants and landed families around Durham City. I'm often at my research in the Benedictine library next to the cathedral.'

'Interesting. And the nature of your research?' the vicar asked.

'History. This is the county of three rivers, the land granted by King Guthred of York in 883 so that the bones of Saint Cuthbert can sleep safe at its heart.'

'So long ago. None but scholars remember Cuthbert; particularly now saints are out of favour with our king,' the vicar said.

Tom snapped the beef rib he chewed on and growled a response, 'The Lindisfarne hermit be not forgotten. At Flodden we marched proud behind his banner.'

Master Burgoyne snorted. 'The Earl of Surrey commanded you. A Howard, a Plantagenet supporter. His breed is also out of favour.'

Ralph slapped the table so hard that the jollity at the far end of the feast died away. 'Maybe so, but Tom is right. The people of Durham County Palatine are the Haliwerfolk. Those who guard the holy man. They are rightly proud of it, and they revere their charge. I'll show you the Guthred evidence if you call on me at the library, whenever you visit the shrine of the Saint.'

'Thank you, I most certainly will —'

The buxom woman at Ralph's side blurted out: 'We live close by the cathedral. High up. We can peer down on the wild geese that beat along the river Wear. I'm Mary. Ralph's my husband, and I'm Tom's other sister. The din outside is from our bairns. They romp with their cousins.'

'You are blessed by the Lord. A bold household this.' The Vicar hiccoughed and swayed in his chair. He held out his goblet for more claret, but his hand wavered and his eyes glazed over.

A yeoman's thick fingers prised free the goblet while other leathery hands supported and guided the weight of the priest's body on its limp slide to the floor.

Master Burgoyne made his way home asleep in musty straw. His horse, tethered to the rear of the cart, paced behind with a lightened back. The priest's twitches and mumbles passed unheard by the farmer at the reins, and by the wife snuggled against her man's shoulder.

Arm in arm, beneath a sleepy rookery, Tom and Rachel stood at their gate and watched the cart mount the rise and slip from sight on its way to the village.

Rachel shuddered. 'Once his head clears, will the Vicar return with his questions?'

'He'll be back. But he'll be more affable, now he's sampled our wine. Have you found time to inspect the book I brought from market?'

'It is indeed Hebrew. The *Book of Zohar*, though not of the hand that penned the version my father lost when we fled Portugal. I'll search for the references to rebirth.' She squeezed his arm. 'But, don't forget the news. I must attend the lawyer in London. Father's friend, Alvaro, bequeathed me a purse equal to ten years of our land's income. Our home is rich in children; his bequest will secure their future.'

'Twelve days on horseback or an uncertain voyage by sea.' Tom reached around her shoulder and drew her close. 'Either way, there's risk.'

'I know of it. Twice I travelled the North Highway alongside my father, from London to within sight of Scotland.'

'I mind your father hired Lincoln guards for your last journey. But since then, twenty-three years have swallowed our youth.'

'Hmm, my husband considers me too worn out to face a paltry two-hundred miles.' She punched his arm with the knuckle of her forefinger.

Tom grabbed her around the waist and squeezed. 'You're yet a filly and too desirable to let out of my sight. I'll ride at your stirrup. And I'll find us a brace of good guards now that men don't give me the wide berth of former days.'

'Thomas, think what stands unprotected here. We need guards for our family and home.' She pulled away, shivered and tightened her shawl against the night wind. The ash trunks blushed plum red as the sun slipped behind the rookery.

The guests had departed, and a satisfied quiet pervaded the Fleck hearthside. Oblivious to the noise of children above the beamed ceiling, Ralph Warren dozed in a chair by the glowing logs. His wife Mary, and her half-sister Hilda, fussed upstairs, putting the young ones to bed. Kate Fleck reclined on a sheepskin beside her mastiff, cooing and fondling his wrinkled face and drooped ears.

Captain Jackson knelt at the hearth and arranged two fresh logs, his white hair illuminated by a fiery halo. At the rattle of the door latch, he stood.

Hilda entered, in the act of pulling off her wimple. Silver-streaked copper locks fell around her shoulders. Mary followed close behind, wimple in hand, silver-flecked yellow curls strewn across her full bosom. 'All done. The wrigglers are in bed — for the time being. They're like a skep of bees in thunder. Fuss and bother. I've threatened to strap them in.'

Ralph opened one eye. 'Ah, the beauty of twilight, when women let their tresses fall. The children are cousins, all of an age. They'll remember these visits, life-long. If needed, I'll climb the stairs and glower at them.'

'You, husband? Glower? You couldn't scare a dove from a damson tree.' Mary flounced across the room and plumped onto his knee. His fingers dived into her armpits. She shrieked, grappled his arms and pinned them to his sides.

Hilda leaned into her husband's chest. 'Does Edward Jackson sometimes wish he'd not wed the quiet maid?'

He squeezed her slim waist, kissed her ear, and murmured, 'By fiery hair you keep me enchanted and bound.'

'And when it's grey?' she asked.

'A swan be a swan, whatever the shade.'

'I once slept on straw in a cow byre where bats flittered. How I gained a man like you is a wonder.' She rested her head on his shoulder and stared into the fire.

The outer door closed with a thud and a sliding of bolts. Rachel and Tom entered the warm room and stood with shoulders touching. The group around the hearth noted Rachel's pursed lips.

'Sad news came this forenoon. Father's friend and employer, Alvaro Jurnet, has left the world. I'm due a portion of his will. We must journey to London. We'll be away a month, or six weeks at most; but there's household and farm to protect.'

'We'll stay here and care for the children, won't we, Ralph?' Mary blurted out.

'Er . . . yes. My students are easy-going and it'll be a chance to escape the Priory and its monkish ways. The fine days linger and Durham can wait. I shall wander the shore and commune with the waves.'

Edward Jackson placed his hand on Tom's shoulder. 'I'll plan for next year's lambs. As usual we'll share the best tups and I'll make sure they mark the ewes. With your permission, I'll choose the sire rams this year. We share boundaries. It's no hardship for me. Your stock will thrive like my own. Make your journey, my friend.'

Hilda's green eyes sparkled. 'And wonderful to have Mary close by.'

'You'll need guards you can trust,' Edward said. 'Two militiamen are shepherds at Elwick Grange, they're nephews of mine. They've known hot trade with raiders on the Tweed. You'd best hire men with such experience, even though you'll meet a milder type of ruffian south along Ermine Street.'

'Yes, I know them. I'll ride over there in the morning.' Tom heard snuffles and broke away to kneel by Kate's side. 'You're troubled, honey. Why the tears?'

'If I'd been made a man, life would be different — and if I knew light. I want to come on your adventure.'

'I'm sorry. The London road is hard. After we return, I promise you'll ride with me to Durham City, or perhaps Newcastle.'

'What can Durham do? If there is a cure, the London physicians will know it.' She rubbed the heel of her palm across her eyes. 'I'm sick of the dark! What's to become of me as I grow old here?'

4

Fog

The same day. October 1536. The Dover Straits.

The old ship, a North Sea cog, rocked on the slow heave of a fog-bound sea. She mumbled in the tones of a contented matron, with quiet grunts and whispers, small clicks and suckings. With each sway of her hull the mainsail gave a feeble flap. Each swell shook the yard and shrouds so that rivulets of condensed mist fell onto the shoulders of the crew, a little group of northerners who squatted on deck and spooned breakfast porridge between uncombed whiskers. A few cables to starboard, cries of seals tolled like the bells of fog-blind ships. Below the bare feet of masthead lookouts, grey murk veiled the deck and streamed through the rigging.

Isaac Fleck shivered. He'd straddled the yard for an hour. His young buttocks ached. Oh, for the broad back of a pony. Better to spread his rump across a mare, behind a gang of his father's cattle, than squat on this shifting timber for a dog's wage. He wiped droplets from his thin beard and glanced at his fellow lookout on the other side of the mast.

'Francis.'

'What now, brother?'

'When d'you reckon we'll see Flanders?'

'Not this day, Isaac. Not this day.'

Below them, a door creaked. Then a yell, 'Keep yer eyes wide, and yer lugs pricked. Them seals sound like they're beached.' The door slammed shut.

Isaac eased his numb thighs. 'I'm baffled how the skipper hears owt through them shaggy old lugs.'

'Keep your voice down. The master's not deaf.'

'Aye, but what's his navigation like? Suppose we're lost.'

Francis coughed and spat into the mist. 'Ben Hood well knows we've drifted south. These waters worry him.'

'Aye, but listen . . . Apart from seals, if such they be, there's nowt but hush. No slap of wave on rock. What's here to scare the man?'

'There's no rock, bonny lad. There's summat else down here to free-up a man's bowels.'

In a swish of wings, a herring gull dropped out of the fog and took up station on the tip of the mast. The white bird flung back its head and tore the silence with a shrieking laugh. They waved their arms and the gull fled. It swooped low across the bows towards a radiance.

Francis seized the mast, pulled himself upright on the yard, and pointed. 'Ahead! See that?'

The gull hung, suspended in silhouette against a haze of gold. The light became an orb. It shimmered for a few breaths, then shrank as though hauled away by wraiths.

Isaac's dark eyes grew wide. 'They say the drowned beckon us from Hell with a lamp.' He met his brother's fierce blue gaze with a sheepish grin, and braced himself.

Francis gave a snort. 'Get away, young'un! With ideas like that you'll never make old bones.'

They peered below to where their shipmates, Jack Punder and Kit Horsley, sat licking out their bowls.

Francis called down, 'Deck there! She thins. Rouse the master.'

Captain Hood heaved his old limbs up the rope ladder of the shrouds. At the mainsail yard he shoved Francis Fleck aside and slung a beefy thigh across the wet timber. He wiped his forehead and stared around. His breath rasped, 'Too far south. Blasted sea fret! Sun, I need thee. Come on, stir thyself.'

Seldom did his appeals to the sky yield fruit, but today he grunted when a breeze flicked at his beard and the sail rippled. The wall of fog sprang to life and swirled along the hull. He urged it on until it thinned, flushed a sudden gold, then vanished. To larboard and starboard, and mere inches above water, acres of level sand glistened. North and south, sand bars stretched on either side until lost in mist. Black and white birds stood in ranks across the rippled sand. They continued to preen even when the ship unveiled before them.

He bellowed, 'We're among the Goodwins! It's the Ship Swallower!' He swung his bulk onto the shrouds and slid downwards while the sail's patched hemp slapped hard against the mast. His boots thudded to the deck. 'Dig out the mate!' The sail took the breeze and filled its belly. The ship answered with a dip of her bows, but the swollen canvas spilled its air and collapsed. Ben Hood spread his boots to counter the next lurch of the deck. 'Look alive! Man the sheets while the wind makes up her mind. Fog bank ahead. Lead line out. Helm, keep midships.'

The mate eased his wiry, bow-legged frame through the hatch and faced his captain. 'A deal of fuss over a bit o' sea fret. It's my watch below. I'd barely nodded off. Can't a man take his rest?'

Ben Hood fixed the mate with a fierce glare. 'I want you on deck. The world knows you've commanded your own ship, Mister Skerry, but you lost her and I intend to keep the *Plenty*. These shoals are stuffed wi' wrecks. They've a death grip, and I've no wish to end my days abed with conger eels.'

Christopher Skerry lowered his eyes and touched his forelock. 'Where do you want me?'

'On the focs'le. I want soundings. You mark the man on the lead line. I'll take station by the helm.' He stamped up the aftercastle ladder as the *Plenty* lurched into another fog bank.

The deck of the venerable cog shifted beneath his boots. He loved her. She'd nosed into estuaries and harbours around the shores of the German Ocean and the Baltic for a man's lifetime. He'd grown old with her.

In a cradle on the margins of Hartlepool's tidal bay, shipwrights had fashioned her hull with adze and borer. They'd used oak throughout: dense, cold-climate oak, from the limestone denes of their native coast. Sad wrecks beneath the cliffs of the ancient town provided her tackle and anchor.

She groaned in a swell, but she held. Years ago, she'd known flame when some oaf built up the galley stove too high in a gale and hot embers tumbled across the deck. The cargo of Baltic pitch had blazed and bubbled from split casks. He'd fought for her when molten blackness slithered and oozed around the hold. The pitch hardened into a wrinkled skin (you could still make out the lumps where it entombed the rats) and it stuck fast even now. She'd survived in a storm of curses and buckets of seawater. Her black bowels kept the auld lass alive, the shipworm's jaw had no tooth for Stockholm tar.

She might sail the seas forever. But her sort were now as scarce as saints. Such archaic design was out of favour. 'Too cumbersome,' the merchants reckoned. 'Manoeuvred worse than a six-gang ox-cart and easy prey for sea-robbers.' Now the ship builders of England launched nimbler vessels; ships with two, and three masts. Ships to stretch out more canvas than the one-masted *Plenty* could ever bear. But what did shore-side men know? Her seasoned old planks would see them out.

His own build served him well too, save for the last few years. Now, his joints complained. His knees clicked when he climbed the mast, and his frame grumbled like mooring ropes on an ebb tide. His shins ached with the sailor's curse: the veins stood out, twisted and knotted like rigging set by drunks.

'Ship!' Isaac Fleck wiped mist from his eyebrows and stared. 'Bare masts off the starboard quarter!'

Ben Hood hauled himself up the shrouds again. 'Pox this muck. I see nowt. Whereabouts? Show me.'

Isaac pointed. 'I caught sight of her, yonder. Through a hole in the fog. Masts.'

'Masts? More than one, then?'

'Aye, two, maybe three. She's bigger than us. Look there. An arrow-shot distant. Where it's thin.'

Ben Hood whistled low. 'Three masts right enough, and rigged like a caravel. By the lean of her sticks, I'd say she's aground. You've sharp eyes, lad. How many on deck?'

'None. Though I swear summat moves on her stern.' Muffled barks and squeals drifted through the gloom. 'A dog. Nowt but a dog.'

'Keep watch.' The skipper slid down the shrouds and bounded onto the deck. He stamped and cursed, spat on his palms and rubbed them together to relieve a touch of rope burn. 'Mister Skerry! We've a stranding, starboard. This easterly shall take us close. Keep on with soundings. What depth now?'

'By the mark, three. Sandy bottom.' the leadsman sang out from the bow. Eyes strained into vapour. 'By the mark, three.' The *Plenty* drifted through the grey swirl. 'By the deep, one!'

'Stand by anchor!' Hood yelled, too late.

The *Plenty* gave a shudder and lurched to a halt. The mast whipped. The man on the lead-line tumbled into the sea, still holding the rope. On the yard, the Fleck brothers sprawled forward to grab at the shrouds and clung there until the swaying ceased.

The mate grabbed a stay and glared at his captain. 'That's more than a touch. She's rammed the shoal. She's aground!'

'Is that a fact, Mister Skerry? Cast the anchor anyway. She'll lift on the tide. Fish that man out of the water. Lookouts back on deck. Ready to lower the yard. Prepare the shore-boat. I want two torches, well primed and lit.'

The captain dived into his cabin. He emerged moments later with a buckled-on sword. 'Flecks to me. Isaac, fetch an axe. Francis, a half-pike.'

Ben Hood eased his broad rump into the stern of the coble and held aloft a tar torch. He eyed Isaac and Francis on the oars. 'Pull away steady. Land me by the wreck. Have a care, though. In this fog we must keep sight of the *Plenty's* torch.'

Isaac and Francis Fleck, hardened farmers and part-time fishermen, pulled together until the bows of the eight-foot craft rasped into the sandbank. Isaac leaped ashore with rope, mallet and stake. Six blows drove the stake deep enough to a make a mooring post.

The master clambered over the bows and waded ashore. He scanned the shallow dome of sand; noted where the coiled casts of lugworms speckled a rippled surface. 'No boot's trod here this tide and I see no crew on that deck. Nowt, apart from that blasted dog and its din.'

Francis spoke up, 'Could be a trap.'

'I doubt it; not on the Ship Swallower. Here's no spot for such games. Even so, we'll take care.' He wiped a drip from his nose. 'Isaac, come with me, and bring the axe. Francis, stay by the boat and keep the pike to hand.' He looked around. 'If we be taken, don't wait. Row back to the *Plenty*, free her by whatever means, and clear out of here.'

Forty paces across quaking sand brought them to the caravel. Streams of mist wreathed the long black hull. The master took hold of a dangling rope and attempted to climb. He gave up. 'Aboard there! What folk aboard?' He waited. No response came, except a faint whine. 'Seems like the dog's in command.' He lifted a foot. 'Help me climb her side. There's nowt for boots to grip. She's carvel built.'

Isaac supported the offered sea-boot with clasped hands. He heaved the master up the smooth hull and over the rail, and then followed. The dog, tethered to the stern mast, cowered and rolled her eyes. 'Now then, bonny lass; who left you all alone?' Isaac approached and held out an arm for the dog to sniff.

'Forget the cur, man; get on with the search. Look in the cabin aft and I'll check the focs'le.' Ben Hood stopped to stare at the deck. 'There's a slick of blood here.' He pushed his thumb through the gore and sniffed at the tip. 'Not a day old.' He glanced around. 'We'd best stay sharp. You keep a grip of that axe.'

Isaac gaped at the dark red spatter. 'Is it human blood?'

'Aye, mebbe ... unless they've supped on goat. Get on and check the cabin.'

Isaac found the door ajar. The sea-bleached panel hung from one hinge, as if wrenched open. A salt-crusted window hardly lifted the gloom within. His scalp bristled at a muffled cough. On a low bunk, a booted foot stuck out from one end of a pile of blankets and a leather-clad head from the other. Isaac stared into a pair of half-open eyes set in an elegantly barbered face.

'Hello. Are you sick?' His voice wavered.

'*Pirata. Mouro.*' The voice came from a rattling chest.

'A pirate raid? What ship is this?'

'*Encantador*. Portugal. *Filho* gone, men gone, senhora gone. *Mouro. Corsario.*'

Isaac brought to mind scraps of Portuguese taught by his mother. He laid a palm on the man's forehead and sensed a feverish heat. 'You are ill or hurt, injured, *ferida*?'

'No hurt. *Peste*. Plague *peste*. Pirata *assustar-se,* afraid *peste*. Take men. Take *filho*.'

Ben Hood's bulk filled the doorway. 'What's this?'

'A sick man. He calls this ship, *Encantador*. She's from Portugal. Moorish pirates dragged everyone away, the women and his son too. They feared to come near this one on account of plague.'

'Plague? Hold your breath and come out of there. Now!'

Isaac glanced towards the bunk, touched his forelock, and squeezed through the door.

Ben Hood glowered. 'Did you touch him?'

'Just his forehead.'

'Shut that door and hold out your hands.' The master pulled the cork from a squat bottle, swigged a mouthful, belched, and then poured glugs over Isaac's palms. 'Rub them together. Spread the liquor about.'

Isaac sniffed his fingers. 'What's this?'

'Portugal brandywine, late of the cargo. Plenty of it. Pirates of the Moorish sort don't pillage liquor.'

'Don't they take a drink?' Isaac feverishly rubbed his fingers.

'Not them. Well, not in public. They declare the blessed fluid to be Satan's broth.'

'And to strip a boat of its people makes for holy work?'

'Bloody religion.' Ben spat. 'I don't hold with such rot. Seamen are best served if they give the blather of priests a wide berth, lest their wits go soft.'

'Owt else in the cargo?'

'Draw them tarpaulins and see for yourself. She's awash with spirit, but there's other delights below. Have a hunt through. The pirates barely touched the cargo. Though, I reckon they'll be back at high water to take the ship.'

Isaac dropped into the hold and heaved crates aside to reveal a layer of straw. He dug deep until he uncovered bundles of six-foot lengths of wood. He gave a whistle.

'What you found, lad?'

'Bowstaves, Captain. Beautiful bowstaves, straight and true. Pure heartwood on one side. With a bit of work they'll make longbows like men bent in the old days.'

'I wonder where they're bound. I've heard King Henry ships them in from Portugal. Pays in gold for quality. Aught else?'

'A lovely smell from sacks of oranges and bags of raisins. Reminds me of Christmas. Firesides and stories and such.'

'Belay the poems! What else?'

'Little wooden boxes; lots of them. They smell good.' He tossed a casket to Ben Hood.

The captain shook the box, opened the hinged lid and sniffed. 'A fortune in spice! There'll be nutmeg, pepper, cinnamon and cloves. Fit for a king's table, and it's come halfway round the world. While I check the hull, you keep an eye out. And keep clear of that Portugueser.' A glow suffused the deck. 'Aye, aye; sun's come to burn the fog off. Aloft you go, and take a look. Keep your voice down.'

Isaac climbed the shrouds of the strange rig and emerged into sunlight. He gazed around under a blue sky. Barely visible, the ocean heaved beneath a white fleece. For miles, the top of the fog shimmered like eider down. To the south, black masts protruded like twigs stuck in white gauze. He called low, 'Masts to the south. A square-rigged two-master and, close by, a fore-and-aft rig with three sticks.'

'How far away?

'Third of a mile. There's a lookout aloft the three-master. He's seen me.'

'Scan around. Any others?'

'Where the fog's thin I see masts and timbers poking out of the sands. They're everywhere. Littered like a ship-breaker's yard.'

'Aye, and a graveyard. She's a hungry bitch, the Ship Swallower. Is the coast in sight?'

'A low fog bank to the east, with hills behind, but they're far off. To the west, much closer, high white cliffs in sunshine, broken by a bay. I see houses on the strand. A little town. Southwest stands a wall of black cloud. The fog's closed in across those ships. I'm losing them.'

'Right. Get down.'

Isaac jumped the final few feet to the deck. 'Do you know those shores, sir?'

'France to the east, Kent to the west. The town you spied will be one of the five old Cinque Ports. Likely, Hythe or Romney.'

'All that wreckage. Where's it from?'

'From hundreds of years of swallowing ships, Isaac. It's no place to linger.'

'What shall we do about those other strandings?'

'Nowt. We get straight back to the *Plenty*. But, afore we shift, we'll gather up a box of brandywine, a bundle of bow-staves and whatever spice we can carry. Load the boat quick and let's clear out.'

Isaac heaved a few bundles, sacks, and boxes out of the hold and then paused. 'The Portugueser — he needs care.'

'Stick a bottle of brandy outside his door, then let him be. I'm not that daft as to ship plague aboard the *Plenty*.'

'The dog ... We'll take the dog.'

'We take nowt off a plague ship. Nowt that's ever drawn breath, that is.'

'I'll cut her tether and let her run free.'

'No you won't. She'll follow us. You can lug this lot to the boat. And quick about it.'

Isaac worked and grunted with the howls of a tethered mongrel in his ears. He fought to keep his mind on hauling salvage.

Francis' face shone with relief to see the outlines of his brother and the master emerge from the fog. They loaded fast and pushed off the sandbank with oars. After a dozen yards the tar torch died in a final sputter.

Ben Hood leaned forward from the stern. 'No matter. I see the *Plenty's* light. Come a bit to starboard. Keep a brisk pace.'

'Tide's on its way out, sir.'

'I know it, Francis. And I know this fog to be a boon, if she holds.'

The fog shifted. Then swirled. Driven before a freshening breeze the murk swept away to the northeast. The shore boat approached the grounded *Plenty* in bright, noon sun. In the shallows around her, the sea was a burnished duck-egg green. Farther out, the surface glowed steel-bright and sparkled with a million ripples. The drying sandbanks threw back white light, fierce to the eyes.

An urgent shout came from the *Plenty*. The rowers bent harder. A hoard of dark shapes undulated across the sandbank. The seals bugled in alarm while they jostled to plunge into the sea. A flock of pied birds lifted in panic before the approach of men who ran full tilt armed with crossbows and spears. The oystercatchers flew overhead, bleating. Urgent hands reached over the side to heave the heavy captain onto the deck of the cog.

Wide-eyed, the mate leaned over the rail and yelled, 'Flecks! Hurry! We need your bows.'

The captain raised a thick finger. 'I'll give the orders, if you don't mind, Mister Skerry. But, on this occasion you are correct. String them bows, and sharp about it! The rest, arm yourselves with pikes and cleavers.'

Isaac and Francis scrambled aboard. Bow staves, full bags of arrows, cords wrapped in oilcloth, together with arm and finger guards, were thrust at them — all the paraphernalia of archers.

They fitted cords to longbows and slung arrow sacks across their shoulders. Francis reached out to his younger brother's bow and flicked at the bowstring. 'Dry enough. Best to forget arm guards and the like. We've no time.'

On the sandbank, the runners halted fifty yards away. Three of them knelt to level crossbows. The others paused and leaned on spears. White turbans and loose robes flared in the sun.

Ben Hood faced his small crew. 'Yon lot in bed sheets are Moors. There's no parley with those pirates. They hunt sailors for the slave market.' He paused to watch his words sink in. 'But, they whimper at sight of their own blood. Make free with your Durham muscle and chop them down. Flecks! Are the bows ready?'

'Aye, captain, ready as might be.' Francis fought to control the crack in his voice. 'Isaac, I'll take the left-hand crossbow and you take the right.'

'My hands shake. I'd not thought to shoot at men.'

'Do as I say! I promised Mam I'd bring you back in one piece.'

Ben Hood yelled, 'Get down!'

Jack Punder fell to the deck with a crossbow bolt in his chest. Another bolt buried its head in the mast and a third swished between the captain and mate. Kit

Horsley crawled to his friend and attempted to staunch gouts of blood by pressing a rag around the bolt.

The captain raised his sword and spat out the words: 'Longbows! Make them pay!'

Francis nodded and spoke with a tremble, 'Nock shafts, Isaac. Remember Dad's words and breathe steady.' The brothers leaned into the bowstaves and drew back cords. His throat grew thick, 'Like Dad said: let your mind's eye see the shafts already in the target.' His voice cleared. 'Draw ... mark ... and loose.' Two clothyard arrows sprang from the *Plenty*.

On saturated sand and in sinking boots, the Moors toiled to rewind their crossbows. Their struggles ceased when shafts slammed into their bent bodies. On the cog, bowstrings thrummed again and hands reached into arrow sacks. The third crossbowman stood erect from his labours. He fell backwards, pierced in chest and shoulder.

'Well marked!' Ben roared out. 'Come on, bloody sea-rovers! If you crave Paradise, now's a grand day for it!'

Yelling, 'Allah Akbar', spears and swords held aloft, the remaining pirates charged across the level sandbank. Archers from childhood, the Flecks' long arms and broad shoulders leaned into longbows and pulled on cords. Every six seconds, their bowstrings sang together. The turbaned runners faltered when two of them sank to their knees, and again when two more fell. Then, as they still advanced, there came the cough and crack of ignited black powder, and lead balls ripped among those still upright. The Moors cried out in alarm, and fled.

'An arquebus?' Ben Hood glanced around amid cheers from his crew.

'From the caravel.' The mate pointed to the stricken black hull. 'There's smoke around her bow. And a man crouched behind the rails.'

5

A Lifting Hull

Ben Hood clung to the shroud tops of his single-masted cog. From his perch he stared across the exposed shoals of the Goodwin Sands and willed the tide to rise. A third of a mile to the south lay the pirate ship — aground like his own. He relaxed at the sight of smoke from their stove and hoped it was a heavy meal. They'd neglected to claim their dead. Fifty yards away, three of their crossbowmen lay where they'd dropped. An evil wagel, a black-backed gull the size of a goose, stood close by about to dine. The eyes would be first. Two swordsmen sprawled twenty yards from the *Plenty*. Francis Fleck and his younger brother Isaac, good archers both, had dashed ashore and salvaged their arrows from the sandbar and the bodies, though not from two wounded who still crawled towards their own ship. The abandoned crossbows and swords might come in handy if they came again. He considered the single arquebus shot that routed the Moors. Perhaps the plague man fired the weapon. It must have been that Portugueser who blasted metal into the pirates' flank. He could not be so ill. Right now though, other matters pressed on him.

A wall of black weather draped the horizon and the sea bore the makings of a swell. Murk hung over the face of the sun. He glowered at the sky, then shivered as though a presence stalked him and his elderly vessel. He longed for high water to lift his ship free before the menace struck. Breakers fringed the southern end of the great Goodwin. Eastwards, the coast of France vanished in rain, and to the west the white cliffs of Kent faded. A swift tide pushed north and shrank the sand banks before his eyes. Soon the flood would burst through the Dover Straits. Then he would turn the threat to his advantage and ride that gathering power.

In contrast to his anxiety, the grey seals lounged indifferent to the coming change. Dozens had heaved ashore and now dozed, head and tail lifted – dark crescents on the sand. He stiffened when one of the beasts stood erect and swayed. The slender female shape took off and sprinted in a stooped fashion toward the beached caravel. The dog set up its damned barking when the running figure seized a rope and appeared to float aboard the black hull. There came a hooting cry and the dog fell silent. His skin crawled; he'd heard a legion of sailors' tales of the Goodwins, and of how the drowned haunted these shoals. Ach! A lot of superstitious blather.

The yard he straddled gave a heave. He lurched and grabbed a rope. The *Plenty* moved! Despite joints that ached, he sped down the mast like a young man.

The mate met him. 'We're shifting, Master.'

'I know it, Mister Skerry. We'll weigh anchor in half an hour. Make the sail ready to shake out. There's new weather in the sou-west, we'll run before the wind once we break free.'

'If we break free,' Skerry muttered.

'What's that? Speak up, man!'

'She's old, tired, and worn-out. Sat half on and half off this shoal can only do her a mischief. I heard a couple of bangs and cracks come out of the hold. I don't care to think of what might be afoot below deck.'

'Those creaks be nowt but a touch of cargo settlement. This cog will take a sand bar, Mister Skerry; she's built for such work.'

'It's the nature of the cargo that concerns me, Master Hood. Such a weight of millstones we stowed at Hartlepool. They'll add up to a load of trouble if they move. We'd have done better to ship less stone and more wool.'

'They're packed around with sand in the normal manner. We've shipped quernstones before without trouble.' He fixed a fierce stare on the mate until the man broke eye contact, but the mate persisted.

'Another matter, Captain, we've lost a man. Jack Punder needs burial. His mates have him sewed up and ready.'

'Not in our best canvas, I hope — if he's to go over the side,' Ben Hood growled.

'Nay, nowt but scraps of worn out stuff. Jack's blood is scrubbed off the deck — though there's a stain to mark his end.'

'When we clear the Goodwins he shall enjoy a proper sailor's burial. Make her ship-shape and secure for sea. We'll tow the shore boat astern.' He scowled to see the mate breathe out and lift his gaze to the sky; insolent dog, he'd have to watch him.

Squalls fell across the Goodwins. The cormorants that had stood in line, black wings outstretched, like crucifixes, gave up the attempt to dry their feathers and joined lines of gulls headed for the shelter of the Kent coast. In a mounting swell the *Plenty* rocked on her bed of sand. With the anchor now stowed snug against the bow and the hull prepared to lift on high tide, the weary crew took the chance to wolf down mutton broth. Indifferent to pulses of rain, Ben Hood paced the deck, hands behind his back. He noted the typical pattern of complaints from his ship's timbers. Perhaps the creaks came louder than usual. He'd beach her when they reached Hartlepool; she needed a scrape down. The bottom dragged yards of weeds and begged for fresh caulk.

A dull thud erupted from below. Seconds later it sounded again, followed by an ugly squeal. Spoons and bowls clattered to the deck and his crew clambered to their feet. The ship yielded up a groan and slumped to larboard. Ben Hood pulled on knots, freed lashings, and wrenched the tarpaulin from the hatch. He gasped at the sight of water. It swilled into the hold from somewhere unseen. It surged between the black quernstones and sluiced away the protection of yellow sand. The querns slipped. The circular basalt shapes slid across one another and rammed apart bales of sodden sheep-wool.

'She's flooded. She's broken!' He stood for a moment like a beaten dog, but then braced his shoulders. 'Right, we'll make for the caravel. There'll be three trips in the shore boat. Gather weapons, the ship's tools, and rations for five days. Fetch the boat to the leeward side. Be sharp about it!'

Someone tugged at his elbow. 'Sir, the caravel's a plague ship!'

'Horsley, take your mucky fingers off my woollens. You've a choice: stay here and drown, swim for the coast, Kent or Calais — whichever you fancy, or take your chance with a minor foreign malady. It's up to you. I want you in the first boat. Make your mind up.' He grabbed his sea bag.

Isaac and Francis rummaged in the stores box for sacks of beans and salt beef, goatskins of water. A flurry of black rats, for once ignored, scampered out of the gloom of the hold to take refuge on the empty aftercastle.

Ben Hood spread his booted feet to find purchase on the tilted deck and called out, 'Load up! Isaac Fleck and Horsley make the first trip with me. Horsley will return for Mister Skerry, Boagey and the elder Fleck, then a last trip for Hart and Knaggs. We'll seize the caravel before the tide gets her. We might find a couple of folk in residence, but let's away!'

Aided by short, curled waves, the stem of the shore boat pitched onto the edge of the vanishing shoal. Burdened with provisions, master and ship's hand waded knee deep across the sandbank toward the black outline of the caravel. Beneath the main mast, a young woman, wrapped in a shawl, backed away when they clambered aboard. The dog stayed close to her skirts and bared its teeth. A ridge of hair stood in a crest along the creature's back.

Ben Hood removed his battered hat and gave a slight bow. 'Shipwrecked seafarers in need of sanctuary. We intend no harm, mistress. You are the runner on the sand?'

The swarthy woman shrank back, her angular features puckered with uncertainty.

Isaac stepped forward. 'Paz. Inglese.' He offered his hand, then thought better of it and tucked it behind his back. The woman nodded and searched his eyes. Her face calmed and she smiled through the start of tears. A torrent of Portuguese burst from her lips. The dog relaxed and crept forward to sniff at Isaac's leggings.

'Captain, meet Maria. She suffered ill-use from the Moors, but escaped and hid by lying flat among the seals.'

'A clever lass, then.' Ben Hood set down his load and glanced at the mainmast shrouds. 'I note you spout the Portuguese prattle, Fleck.'

'Aye, a smattering. And Francis too.'

'How come?' Ben Hood bounced his weight on the deck planks.

'Around our mother's skirts.'

'Oh, aye? Such might come in handy. Can you educated Flecks also sail a Portuguese caravel?' He stood back and surveyed the three masts.

'We've no such experience, sir.'

'Aye, well — that matter will soon change. This be a tidy craft. Let's hope she floats.'

The last six members of the cog's crew splashed across the bank through a swirl of foam, their boots sucked at by quicksand. Ben Hood met them at the ship's rail.

'Mister Skerry, hold you knowledge of this queer rig?'

'Aye, I've done my share of trips out of the Flandyke Shore in caravels.' He threw his burden onto the deck and clambered aboard.

'And your opinion of the design?'

Christopher Skerry slapped a palm against the mainmast. 'Fore-and-aft rig, narrow hull and butted planks make for speed. In a headwind, the dumpy clinker-built cog gets driven astern, but this beauty will beat close to the wind — handled right.'

'Then, Mister Skerry, until I become better acquainted, you shall be this vessel's sailing master. I remain in command and you report to me.'

The mate sniffed. 'We're too short-handed to fettle the best out of her.'

'Needs must do. Those given to prayer can ask for a fair wind.' Ben Hood surveyed his meagre crew of Hartlepool men, a skinny Portuguese girl, and a brown dog. 'Before you pray, three of you can aquaint yourself with those crossbows, we might yet need them.'

A cracked voice quivered from behind, 'Be there still plague on this boat?'

Ben Hood spun around. 'Ah, Horsley. The plague; in all the excitement it fair slipped my mind. Isaac, have a care for any miasma that's about. Hold your breath when you check on that Portugueser. See if he's dead yet. Though likely he's not, for someone discharged the arquebus. Seeing as you crave cleaner air, Horsley, take yourself up the main mast and keep sharp watch on that pirate. Any movement — yell out!'

Isaac entered the dim cabin with pursed lips and pinched nose. He allowed himself a brief sniff and found the air sweet enough. Once his eyes adjusted, he stared into the iron maw of an arquebus held by the plague man. He gulped. 'Me Inglese. Mouro run.'

'*Bom!* Inglese, good. Bad Inglese comandante want caravela. Me, Senhor Henrique Norte. Tell him caravela *Encantador*, mine.'

'Our ship is broken-backed. We come for refuge. Has your sickness gone?' Isaac asked.

The man coughed and wheezed. 'False *peste*. She come, she go. A man lives. She make *pirata* run.' He cackled out a laugh.

'You scattered them by arquebus. Good shot.'

'And you! *Grande* war-bow. *Admirare!*'

'I go now.' Isaac reached into his belt bag and pulled out a sphere the size of a fist. 'Here is English cheese. *Queijo Ingles*. Eat.' He ducked outside. His brother and Kit Horsley were high in the masts, adjusting the rig. The mate stood below, shouting brisk orders.

Ben Hood fixed him with a baleful glare. 'Is he dead, then? Or do we carry the stink of plague?'

'He's alive, sir, but he's aggrieved. He's sat on a box and nurses his arquebus. He reckons his ailment is but false plague and nowt to worry over, though the signs are bonny enough to make a pirate bolt. He wants you to know this is his ship. The *Encantador* belongs to him.'

'Be that so? And does he reckon we make his new crew?'

'Sir, if he's aboard his own ship we've no right to seize her as salvage.'

'I need no instruction on the laws of the sea, young Fleck. Anyway, what sort of a name be *Encantador*? What's it mean?'

'The Enchanter.' Isaac replied.

'Ah, some sort of Portuguese witch, I suppose. But, she'll do. And while you're doing nowt, fetch sand and cover up yon blood slick.'

Waves set up a rhythmic slap against the *Encantador's* hull. The halyards sang when the first of a series of black squalls struck and drenched the deck. Like a fallen bullock that staggers to its feet, the caravel wrenched free with a low grunt.

'Mister mate!' Ben Hood bellowed. 'Time to show your skill.'

'Aye, aye, Master. You Flecks take the helm. The rest gather round and shake out the mizzen. She's a lateen sail. Careful how she rises. Horsley, undo those cleats. Hoist away!'

To the crew's shouts of, 'Heave! Heave!' the slanted yard creaked up the mast to spill a tan coloured sail into wind off the starboard quarter. The canvas filled and the crew made fast the sheets. The mate noted the lean of the masts. 'Steady now. Larboard helm, hard.' The vertical post that comprised the whipstaff creaked under the weight of Francis and Isaac as it drove the tiller to one side. 'Enough. Hold her there.' He leaned over the rail, stared into the sea alongside the hull, and waited.

Timbers shuddered when the caravel turned, as though on a pivot, swung around to face deeper water and proceeded to rasp and slither off the sandbank. The helm fought its way back to centre. *Encantador* leaned and, after a dozen grinding yards, lifted clear. Within a cable, she touched bottom again and grounded on another shoal. The next swell heaved her up and she slid forward.

'Larboard!' the mate bawled. He bounded to the stern and added his weight to the helm. With a final shudder the black hull plunged into deep water. 'Larboard full!'

The mate's knuckles whitened on the whipstaff, and timbers squealed, as the craft struck a glancing blow to the part-submerged hull of the *Plenty*. He gasped and crossed himself as he witnessed Jack Punder's hemp-wrapped body surface from the wreck in the wake of the *Encantador*. The grey shape bobbed a few times and then sank.

He passed a hand across his eyes, then leaned over the side. 'There's nobbut a scratch or two. A bit close, though. Well done, lads. I'll keep helm with you. We'll pick our way through the shoals 'til we find sea-way. The mizzen gives us all the steerage we need.' He called down into the well of the deck, 'Master! I take it you aim to head nor' by nor'east.'

'You take it right, Mister Skerry, for the reverse course shall deliver us into the arms of the pirate. We need to keep an eye out for him. A rising tide lifts all hulls.'

Now a hundred yards astern, the upturned hull of the *Plenty* rolled over. Her shattered mast thudded onto the aftercastle. Ben Hood's leathery brow puckered and his eyes pricked and teared at the sight of his ancient cog overwhelmed. 'Goodbye, auld lass,' he murmured.

6

Pursuit

At the pace of a strolling lady, the black shape of the caravel threaded between sand bars that stretched for half a league. Lines of breakers slipped past on either side as the hungry arms of the Ship Swallower disappeared beneath foam and blown spume.

After half an hour Ben Hood tapped Kit Horsley on the shoulder. 'Take a trip up the mainmast and tell me what you see.' He watched the seaman climb the shrouds, and waited. He bit another lump out of his thumbnail. He must stop that. The visit of the ache that dragged low in his belly, made him do it.

Horsley called, 'A straight channel ahead. And she widens out.'

'And astern?' He yelled, then held up his thumb, squinted at his chewed nail, and waited.

'Bloody Hell! A three-master. Half a mile off. On our course. She carries a full rig of lateens, and she chews white water.'

'Aught else, Horsley? Just sails?'

After a few moments a cracked yell came from the mainmast top. 'Master! Looks like we've trouble! She's sprouted banks of oars!'

'Has she now?' He felt the stares of his crew. 'Well,' He gave a belch. 'You stay aloft and keep an eye on her.' He rubbed his stomach. A touch of wind in the belly. Nowt but wind.

Senhor Henrique emerged from his quarters and, ashen faced, sidled up, and stood swaying. Ben nodded to the Portuguese and spoke without hope of comprehension, 'You should be in bed, Senhor. But as you're upright you might prepare your arquebus, for we've a pirate stuck to our tail. No doubt some of your own crew are chained to her benches.' He called to the stern, 'Mister Skerry, you stand as sailing master today; will you make sufficient speed to outrun an oared galley?'

'Is there another choice?' The mate squinted into the bright haze astern. Green lateen sails, swollen with wind, approached like a great swimming bird. The splash of oars along her flanks was rhythmic. 'To the foremast, lads. Hoist sail and trim for work. We must grab any flick of the breeze or those oars will make an end of it.'

Ropes hissed through squealing pulleys as the square sail ascended on its oaken yard. The canvas took the wind with a thwack, shook it free, caught it again, and filled. The crew made fast the sheets and the caravel lurched. The thud of the sail vibrated through the helm and the sea foamed around her stem. The mate stared ahead. 'The foresail's full as Henry's royal belly. It's blocked my sightline.' He shouted to the bow, 'Lookout for'ard! Yell out if we start to lose mid-channel.'

'Channel's good,' came the response.

'The lady snatches for a breath of open sea,' Christopher Skerry muttered. He surveyed the lines of broken surf that ran parallel to his course. 'Hoist the mainsail! She's big. Take it steady.'

The great, triangular mainsail filled and the caravel leaned before the wind. The sea hissed along her sleek sides. Ben Hood touched shoulders with the mate. 'Good seamanship, Mister Skerry. But, is it enough? Those devils make three feet to our two.'

'Then we are in need of prayer, seeing as we lack the thrust of oars. That slaver's strayed from her usual waters. I've not heard of a Barbary galley this far north.'

Ben Hood nodded. 'Nor I. But they're a plague in the Mediterranean. Folk aren't safe in their beds along the French shore; they carry off the young of whole villages to their African markets.'

'Well, Captain, they'll not take me without blood.' The mate glanced at the pennant streaming from the mainmast top. 'The wind favours us — but it's fickle. If she shifts too much, I'll need to trim, and we lose way. That's when oars will decide the matter. Let's hope the pirate heels and must close his oar holes to stop a flood; if he does, we'll have a chance.'

Astern, the wave tops curled; the master hawked and spat into the white combs. 'Then I'd best make plans.' He slid down the polished handrails of the aftercastle ladder without his feet touching the rungs. He gathered the Fleck brothers together and laid his muscular arms across their shoulders. 'We need to talk.'

Long minutes passed while the little crew, with anxious glances towards the rising and dipping oars of their pursuer, trimmed sails and put a better edge to their few weapons. Those with experience knew the inevitable, knew the sun's heat would soon fade and the wind shift to press at them from the hills of Kent. The caravel gradually lost way and the oared galley advanced to surge a mere hundred yards astern. Ben Hood gripped the aftercastle rail, the Fleck brothers at his side. The stern of the caravel rose and fell in a following sea. By their legs, on a deck coated in sand, perched a bucket of molten Stockholm tar. It bubbled and spat above a brazier of coal. Nearby, three of the crew gingerly wound tension into the captured crossbows.

'How close do you need him, lads?'

Francis grunted out the answer. 'Close. These tar arrows are out of balance. They're front heavy, short, and we won't make a full draw. Fifty yards will do.'

'Not long now.' The master squinted into the lowered sun. 'Do you see those two heathen perched on her bows? They sport crossbows.'

'Aye, they're winding the handles. On pitching decks, both them and us will struggle to find target. Time to nock arrows, Isaac. We can but try.'

The brothers fitted arrows. Leather sleeves shielded their bow arms from the lash of the bowstring, and tubes of cow horn protected their fingers,

Francis nudged Isaac. 'I'll mark the left-hand one and you mark the right. Remember Dad's advice: let the mind's eye see the shaft already in the target. Together now. Draw ... mark ... loose!'

Two bodkin arrows flew from the stern of the black caravel. The iron warheads thudded into the rising bows of the galley, two more were already in flight and another pair on the point of release. The Barbary crossbowmen made hurried aim, fired and ducked out of sight. Both bolts struck the caravel's mizzen sail, burst through, and pierced the mainsail, where they hung lifeless. The longbow arrows clipped the forward rigging of the galley and spun to the deck.

Francis glowered. 'Too much sea runs today. Dad's words won't hold on a pitching deck.'

Isaac sucked a knuckle skinned by the whip of the bowstring. 'Aye, it worked in the clarts of Flodden, but we've no clay to root our toes in.'

'Still, brother mine, Dad will be prick-eared for our tales when we get back.'

Isaac mumbled, 'Aye, mebbe ...'

Ben Hood hit the rail with his fist. 'Don't fret, your next target's bigger. The gap narrows. I'll give the tar a bit of a stir.'

'We've not tried this afore; I don't know how the longbow will take it.' Francis dipped a cloth-wrapped arrow into the tar bucket. He nocked the arrow and plunged the wrapped bodkin warhead into the brazier. In seconds he held a flaming arrow that dripped molten pitch across the sanded deck. He leaned into the bow and launched the clothyard in a high arc toward the galley. The flames appeared to die while the shaft flew. It struck the centre of the distended foresail and clung there for seconds before blazing into new life.

The captain smacked his palms together, 'Well, I'm blowed. The wind's dried out those sails a treat. See that, Mister Mate?'

'I did, and I'd like another look. Be there more?'

Both longbows delivered fire arrows in pairs until eight burned in a haphazard scatter across the sail. Shrieks came from the galley and a flurry of roped buckets fell into the sea. The beat of the oar drum stopped. The crew, in turmoil, hurled water onto torched sailcloth. The wind pulled a plume of acrid smoke between the two craft. The blaze roared higher until the sail fell in charred and flaming fragments to be stamped on and quenched. The galley lurched to starboard and exposed the helmsman at the stern. Senhor Norte rested his arquebus on the rail, blew on the match, and fired. The kick threw him backwards a pace and the ball flew skywards over the pirate's masts. Kit Horsley loosed his crossbow into the clearing smoke, but the bolt flew wide.

Francis reached into his arrow sack. 'Straight bodkins for him, Isaac. Allow for pitch like we do for wind. Together now.'

The tall Moor released the helm, staggered back and slumped against the guardrail. A second Moor took his place and fell, and then a third. Twenty arrows descended on the galley in the space of one minute. The Barbary vessel, out of control, swung away to starboard.

To screamed orders, the pirates hoisted a tarpaulin across the stern. The helmsman no longer cowered from the arrow storm and brought the bows around to renew the chase. Two Moors strode with raised whips along the central walkway of the deck and flogged the shoulders of men on the benches below. One fell among the oar slaves, an arrow in his back. The galley dropped farther astern.

Ben Hood nudged Isaac's arm. 'See the big'un? He prances around in fancy green coat and turban? He's in the bows now. He lays the lash on the crossbowmen. He'll be the shipmaster.'

Isaac grunted, nocked an arrow, leaned into the bow, and released. Francis shot a second that streaked behind Isaac's with a six-yard gap. The Moor took both clothyards in the chest and collapsed.

The wind slackened and the wave tops no longer curled to break white. The *Encantador* sighed as the belly in her sails collapsed. The oared galley, despite its canvas charred and useless, crept closer to the caravel. Few targets remained for the longbow; the pirates had draped a protective screen of sodden canvas from foremast to the prow. The crew of the caravel gathered to watch the gap narrow. Fingers tightened around cleavers, axes, and half-pikes. Knuckles whitened while they shivered in thick sea clothes.

Ben Hood looked at the drawn faces of his crew. 'Stand firm, my bonny lads. Stand firm and make you ready.' He swung back to face the galley, and cursed. 'There's a man on the foremast. He frees ropes. They're up to summat!'

The screen fell to the deck and a crowd of Moors dragged the tarpaulin away. A dark shape crouched in the bows; its maw gaped and threatened to reach out to each horrified watcher in turn. Ben Hood banged the rail with his fist. 'God's breath. They've heaved a cannon onto the foredeck. Looks like a falconet or a culverin. She could make an end to this. How many arrows left, Francis?'

'We've but twelve between us, Captain.'

'Make them count, and this day shall bear your name.'

The cannon gave a slow, black-powder roar and leapt backwards on its carriage. A broad cone of iron balls swished overhead and tore holes in the caravel's mizzen sail. It ripped onwards through her mainsail and foresail. On the galley, the gun crew made ready for the next discharge. The quencher tried to ram his swab down the barrel, but took an arrow in his back. He twisted around and fell across the quenching rod. The loader shoved the wounded man to the deck and rammed a cartridge of gunpowder down the barrel. A bag of shot followed the powder. He howled, fell sideways, and grabbed at the arrow buried in his thigh. Other corsairs appeared and ran the gun forward into firing position, then retreated. The leveler flinched when an arrow plucked at the folds of his robe. He completed his aim and motioned to the firer who sheltered behind the gun. The firer leapt to one side of the barrel and lowered his match pole. He yelled and applied the match to the touch-hole. Wind, waves, and gulls appeared to freeze while the slow powder fizzed downwards into the barrel. The Moor stepped to one side, covered his ears — and vanished in a sheet of flame.

Lumps of shattered iron raked the pirate deck. A heartbeat later, the boom of the ruptured cannon reached the *Encantador*. Those on her aftercastle made themselves small while hot metal fell from the sky. The surface of the sea hissed and spat.

Henrique Norte jumped to his feet. 'Explodir! Explodir!'

Ben Hood joined him. 'Aye, a welcome burst barrel. Such comes of impatience. She needed time to cool down — and I learn Portuguese. Mister Skerry, I want this vessel checked over for hot iron; we want no fires.' He flinched when the senhor grabbed his arm and shouted a torrent of Portuguese. 'All right, all right, calm yourself down, senhor. What's he say, Isaac?'

'He wants you to put alongside the galley, sir.'

'Is that so? Your opinion, please, Mister Skerry.'

'That explosion cleared the corsair's deck, there's havoc aboard. Her oars are askew and she's dead in the water. We've enough sea room to come about. 'Tis a captain's decision.'

Ben Hood rubbed his belly; that nagging ache again. 'Then bring her about, Mister Skerry. Bring her about.'

7

Stench

The square foresail of the *Encantador* sank to the deck. Hood, Skerry, and Norte, laid their weight and muscle against the six-foot length of the whipstaff. To yells of, 'Sheets to the wind,' the caravel slowed and clawed her way to larboard. The lateen sails of mainmast and mizzen spilled the air, hung lifeless, and then filled from the other side. With swollen sails now pressed against her masts the caravel clawed into the breeze on the first leg of a tack. She ran at an angle for the broken water of a drowning shoal, and she leaned. Ben Hood's knuckles whitened under the strain.

'We're in your hands, Mister Skerry!' he bawled into the mate's ear. 'But don't leave it too late!' He glared at Christopher Skerry and then at the confused, broken water a few cables from the bows.

The nervous deck crew of six hands, from their various stations, stared up at the aftercastle. Will Boagey, on the bows, glanced ahead and crossed himself.

The mate's body stiffened. 'Standby to come about! Have a care when she turns. Knaggs, up here to the helm — give us your weight'. Knaggs bounded up the ladder.

'Come about!' the mate bawled as a gust hit the sails and she heeled.

Four men heaved on the vertical whipstaff, their boots fighting for purchase on the deck. With groans from masts, and squeals of ropes in pulley blocks, the caravel clawed onto her new and final tack.

Like a deerhound, a bleached bone in her teeth, she bore down on the Barbary galley. One white gull held station above her wake. The mate shouted for a lowered mainsail. The yard creaked to the deck, and her speed slackened. The foam around her stem subsided to a delicate lace. 'Percy Hart, get you to the shrouds!' the mate yelled.

Ben Hood watched his crewman ascend the mast and judged it time to take back command. 'Lookout! How be the pirate's deck?'

'Captain! Bodies in the for'ard end, not one left upright. Blood everywhere. The deck's open down the centre. A crowd of men below. Draped over the oars. They gawp up at me. Some wave. They've shipped oars!'

'Mister Skerry, fenders over the side, then grapple her fore and aft. Senhor, charge your arquebus, and cover me.' Ben Hood eased his sword belt.

A crewman on the forecastle swung a grappling iron around his head and let it fly. The metal claws hooked the galley's stern rail and he heaved on the line. The mate did the same from the *Encantador's* aftercastle and grappled the pirate's foredeck. Ben Hood unsheathed his sword and pointed its tip at the galley. 'Pull us in steady, but watch out for devils. Make fast with a hitch in case we leave in a rush.'

The vessels closed and thudded together. Timbers squealed in protest whilst hulls chafed, rose and fell, with the heave of the sea. The crew stared and tightened their grip on pikes and bows. He choked back a retch. 'God! Such a reek from her!' He faced the crew. 'Steady now, lads. Guard those few arrows. Horsley and Knaggs, follow me with pikes. Keep sharp, and cover my back.' He jumped onto the deck of the pirate and raised his sword. 'I take this ship!'

A clamour of voices rose up from beneath his feet. Through the long, open hatch of the oar deck, scores of startled eyes stared back from the dark heart of the galley. Haggard eyes of begrimed and bearded men. Men in rags. Rows of them. The clamour died away and he calculated their number in silence: three to an oar, twenty oars — sixty men. He gagged again, at the stench.

An arquebus erupted, and he spun around. Ten feet away a corsair slumped to his knees, a whip in one hand, a curved blade in the other. The man fell forward, his clothing rent, his turban flushed with crimson. Behind a mast, Horsley struggled to free the hooked blade of his pike from the mail-covered shoulder of another corsair while Knaggs drove the point of his own into the man's throat. The pirate staggered, coughing to the rail, and fell between the hulls at the instant a swell thudded them together.

Ben Hood scanned the litter of crumpled Moors. Apart from the wide-eyed and panting Horsley and Knaggs, he stood alone on the deck of the galley. Broken bodies lodged against hatch covers and piles of rope, wherever the cannon burst had flung them. He beckoned to the rest of his crew who lined the rails of the *Encantador*. 'Quick, lads, over here with your half-pikes.'

The sailors leapt the gap between the two hulls and boots thudded to the deck. 'Skipper! It's not done yet.' Isaac yelled.

'Bastardo!' The scream came from the stern. A knife in his back, and the jaws of a brown dog clamped to his elbow, a blond haired pirate crashed against the rail. The slender Portuguese girl wrenched free the blade and thrust it again between his ribs. 'Bastardo!' She kicked him in the groin and shoved until he fell over the side. She raised the dagger and, with blood to her elbow and eyes that bulged, swooped into the cabin. A few breaths later she ducked from the cabin and flourished a hefty iron key. Cheers and shouts in a clutch of languages greeted her leap to the oar deck. Isaac leapt after her wiry body. Gradually, to the rasp and clatter of chains, sixty broken men climbed from their tomb in the hold.

'Captain, we'll get trouble from this lot, and their stink makes me heave.' Christopher Skerry glowered at the throng of ragged men. Men from a dozen lands crowded the long deck of the galley. Ben Hood and his ship's mate stared down from the wreck of the forecastle. 'We've Englishmen among them, and there's Irish.' Skerry paused for breath. 'There's Scotch, Frenchies and Spaniards. A couple of Danes. There's others too — heathen-heads from God knows where.'

'None of them stink as bad as your Whitby ginnels, Mister Skerry. More important, at least twenty white men, a couple of women, a clutch of Africans, and one dog, have shipped with the caravel. The senhor has recovered his crew. See how the fine gentleman gives out orders and makes ready to sail. Where do we stand now?'

'On the deck of a Barbary corsair. On congealed blood is where we stand. And no cargo to fetch a profit — unless we take up slaving.'

'Aye, but yonder we've a prospered crewman. He's taken on a servant.' He shouted above the gabble of voices, 'How now, young'un?'

At the foot of the foremast, an immobilised Isaac Fleck stared down onto the glistening shoulders of a huge African. The man knelt on the deck, muscular ebony arms wrapped around the Englishman's rumpled stockinged legs. 'He grabbed me and won't leave off, sir. I only chucked him a lump of cheese.'

Ben Hood spat over the side and grimaced at the mate. 'We've an oared galley and a cargo of slaves. The market for such be on the Coast of Barbary. I've no wish to poke around that shore, make no mistake.'

'Nor me, captain. But we've a cargo of strangers. By the look of some, I'd not have easy nights. We might put them ashore somewhere — if they don't cut our throats first. Once we're rid of them, we could ship oars and sail our prize home. This hull looks well fashioned. Built of precious Atlas cedar. She's light, swift, and slow to rot. We've caught a rare bird and good might come of it yet. And the crew expects a share of the prize.'

'Seems you have it all worked out, Mister Skerry.'

'And I've worked out why two of the pirates had yellow hair, and why this galley was so far north. Dutchmen brought her here.'

'Dutchmen in league with the Barbaries?' Ben Hood spat over the side. 'I don't care much for the world these days.'

'Captain. Senhor Norte comes aboard.' The call came from Isaac, in the process of extricating himself from the embrace of the African.

'Then pull alongside of me and make ready your Portuguese lingo.'

'*Amigo*. Henrico Nortes, *agradecido*.' Senhor Norte now sported a blue velvet doublet and matched hose. He grasped Ben Hood's massive hands and held them. Words poured from him, and a tear trickled into his beard. He touched the head of a slender boy at his side and boomed out, '*Capitao* Benjamin, *este homem filho* Benjamin. Benjamin. *Agradecido*.'

The captain freed his hands. 'Translate the gentleman's blather, Isaac. He's no doubt pleased, but why keep shouting my name?'

'Benjamin means youngest son, sir — or son of my old age. The lad is another Benjamin; he's so called because he's the senhor's last son. The father is full of gratitude for your courage today.'

'Well I'm blowed! Benjamin, son of my old age, eh? I never knew such.'

'It's writ in the Bible, sir. Benjamin was the youngest of Jacob's twelve sons.'

'Twelve sons? He must have been worn out.'

'Aye, and Benjamin himself fathered ten .'

'How do you Flecks come by all this learning?'

'We've a scholar for a mother.'

The mate coughed and broke in, 'Captain, the senhor bears a gift.'

'Oh aye? And what might this be?' His hand dropped beneath the weight of the small leather bag. He stiffened when Senhor Norte grasped his shoulders and kissed him on both cheeks. In one movement, the Portuguese father and son stepped back and, with a flourish of capes, bowed low to the Englishman. They swung around and leapt onto the deck of the caravel.

Grappling lines released, the vessels parted company. Both drifted northwards, their crews taking stock beneath a sky torn by wind into shreds and patches. Norte gave one last salute and called out, '*O Tamisa!*' The *Encantador's* sails filled and she leaned like a gypsy dancer. She set a course for the Thames estuary across a bruise-coloured sea with white water around her prow. Ben Hood gave a casual salute, his attention focussed on his latest set of masts. He gazed aloft, deaf to a series of yells and splashes while the freed slaves, with violent insults, flung the Corsair dead and wounded overboard, among them a second fair-haired man. A three-knot tide funnelled up the English Channel and now squeezed through the Straits of Dover. Little margin remained and it grew dark.

'Mister Skerry, our decks be ship-shape enough. Take us clear of the Goodwins while this tide runs. We've an hour before slack water. You did well to replace the damaged sails. Now take us north. Once free of the shoals, bear northwest towards the Kent coast. I intend to stand two miles off the North

Foreland cliffs and from thence into open water. On no account let her run east. I don't crave parley with the French; I've had a belly-full of foreigners today.'

'Captain, we've upwards of thirty extra men on deck. Men not from Hartlepool.'

'Ah, yes, they're a bit of a clutter, but a happy lot now they've drowned the Barbaries. We set out short-handed, but the crew's multiplied like fleas on a dog. Where are those Flecks?'

Francis, and Isaac, a large African between them, pushed through the throng to reach Ben Hood.

'You two have a way with foreigners; I want you to coax those oarsmen back to the benches. Tell them they're free of chains, and ask politely if they've strength for a bit more rowing. We'll feed them when we've worked out the victual arrangements on this particular craft.'

Francis spoke up, 'We've talked with the men already. Some of them took the lash on those benches for a year or more. They share a dog's dinner sort of language that works across tongues —'

Isaac interrupted. 'That's right, sir.' He rested a hand on the African's huge shoulder. 'And this man's done three years on galleys. He's convinced the others that they're no longer slaves and won't come to harm.'

Ben Hood looked the African up and down. 'You speak English, Mister African?'

The response rang out, deep and resonant, 'Name, Dayo. It say, joy comes. Me, Yoruba man.' He slipped his hand into Isaac's and gave a nod to the captain. 'Isaac, new brother. Free men take oar for you.'

Ben Hood coughed. 'Brother, eh? Well that's grand. A ship can't have too many Flecks in the crew. I place you three in charge of the oar deck. See what needs fettling and put it right. The sky's clear, a cold night to come and we've a shoal of empty bellies. I want Knaggs to cobble together a hot stew of some sort.' The shipmaster glanced around at the activity of his sailing crew then headed for the stern cabin.

The air in the cabin of the Corsair master caused Ben Hood's nose to wrinkle. While his eyes adjusted to the gloom, he scanned the triangular space. Embroidered green cloths festooned the bulkheads. An oriental carpet of intricate floral weave covered the deck and a velvet cushion rested at one end. He pulled back blankets of fine merino wool to expose a thick mattress on a low bunk. He prodded the bed and muttered, 'Filthy sea-wolf. The bloody heathen's set up like the madame of an Ostend brothel.'

Knuckles rapped on the half-open door. 'Captain, sir. Knaggs here. There's salt beef, smoked mutton, dried fish, peas, cabbages and onions, and lots of round, yellow and juicy fruit I've not seen afore. Enough to make a broth.'

'Then sharp about it, man! Do whatever's quickest. Keep the oranges apart, we don't want them in the pottage.'

'Aye, cap'n. But I have to tell ye there's a nanny goat bleating in a pen below deck. Mebbe you'd fancy fresh meat?'

'No! Let the creature bide in peace, I've seen enough slaughter for one day. Anyway, she'll doubtless be a milker. Chuck her a cabbage with my compliments.'

'Aye, aye, sir.'

'Hang on, Knaggs. Hold your arms out.' Ben Hood ripped the cloth hangings from the bulkheads and threw them through the door; he followed with the two cushions. 'You can keep those, along with any fleas they carry.'

'Thank ye, cap'n, sir. They'll make someone's eyes a bit fonder back home.'

'Away wi' thee. And don't take forever with the victuals.'

Ben Hood ripped the carpet from the deck and slung it outside. He did the same with the blankets and beat them against the rails. He gave the mattress a few kicks along the deck until feathers leaked, then flung it back inside. It hit the bunk board with a thud. He halted the next kick when a square panel fell away from the bulkhead to expose a chamber. He dived forward to grope in the gloom and pulled out a clutch of leather bags, each one bound at the neck. He grunted and closed the cabin door, slid the bolt home and opened the window shutter.

Low, evening light showed a following sea and the first signs of stars. The galley made a good clip; the masts creaked before a southwest wind and the splash of oars set up a comforting beat. A sound ship made him happy, the pain in his belly had gone to sleep, and his life held new interest. Now for the Moor's secret.

He untied a bag and spilled a river of silver onto the mattress. Weird squiggles covered the coins. He spat on one, rubbed the turbaned face with his calloused thumb, and gave a grunt of satisfaction. The next two bags also held silver: Spanish coins, French, Danish, Hanseatic, and others unknown. The fourth bag held only English coin; he chuckled to find the image of bloated Henry set to one side. The Moors are no fools, he mused; the turbaned men well know the Tudor king's trick of debasing his coinage with cheap metal. The last two bags yielded brilliant streams and brought a gasp. Pure gold coins of Portugal, Spain, Genoa, and Venice glittered before him. Soft and low, he whistled a dimly remembered childhood skipping tune while he bagged up the hoard

.

8

Ermine Street

Tom Fleck's party, wrapped in cloaks, set out from Crimdon Hall on strong horses. Two burly guards, brothers in breastplates and helmets, led the way, vertical spears slotted into saddles. His wife and daughter, their horses linked by a rope, rode behind the guards. Kate's own guard, her brown mastiff, paced alongside the lass's gelding. He took up the rear; short-sword at his knee and longbow on his back. He planned on thirty miles today. With dry weather the journey south would take ten days, barring lame mounts, sickness and strife.

He caught the smell of Stockton before they entered the village. Powdered cattle dung swirled across the beaten track; drovers had been through here. His womenfolk pulled the sides of their wimples across their mouths. The mastiff sneezed.

The reek of human and animal waste recalled a day, twenty-three years earlier. Driven by bloody-minded rebellion, he'd fled through here to escape service with the lord of the manor's militia. He'd quailed at the sight of hostile eyes that stared from window holes hacked into the crude walls of low cottages. Village curs, the pets of no man, had broken off their forage of a midden to rush at him. He'd driven them off with his quarterstaff. He'd spoken with the one person abroad on this same street. She'd had trouble driving a skittish cow and calf to common pasture. He'd helped her. A sweet but skinny lass, she'd a rattle in the chest. She'd be long dead.

Rare, the glints of sun that sodden year. He'd fought Mark Warren at the ford on the Tees. He'd felled that lord of the manor's son and almost drowned the rapist bully. He'd fled across the river with his wounded dog. They'd hurried through the salt marsh and stumbled into this village. He cherished Meg's descendants, but of all his dogs she was the cleverest, the most faithful. He'd not foreseen how they'd come to cower together from cannon shot, and shiver with fright, on a hillside a bare five miles from Scotland. Steady rain all day, slippery mud. The clatter of arrows on massed pikes. Fifteen-thirteen grew into a grey and ill year. The corn drowned and good men died that September.

Today, the sky shone blue, shot across with veils of milk-white. A pair of fork-tailed kites circled overhead, their attention fixed on the middens. Today, the compacted mud and dung surface of Stockton's high street shimmered. The sun drew foul vapours from its cracked clay. A pack of dogs surrounded the eroded market cross. They ignored him this time and stared with slavering intent at a hissing cat marooned on top of the stone pillar. To the right, goats picked among a litter of cabbage stumps strewn outside an alehouse. By a pigsty, a clutch of ragged urchins chanted and raised a cloud of dust. They took turns to jump in and out of a whirling rope. A score of bare feet pounding out a skipping game.

His party drew alongside a woman who carried a basket and leaned upon a stick. At their approach she twisted around with a flicker of hope in her eyes.

'Good forenoon, masters.' She lifted a cloth from her basket. 'New baked mutton pies, but one farthing apiece. They're hot from the oven.'

Tom looked down into her lined, angular face. She met his gaze with a start of recognition. Her eyes widened.

She spoke in a faint voice, 'Do I know you from the past, sir? Is it truly John Smith?'

Tom dismounted and placed a hand on her shawled arm. 'I might be. I did tease you with that name, but I recall you claimed Henry Tudor as your title that day.' He laughed.

She hesitated, glanced up at Rachel, then continued, 'And you gave me a silver penny with the real Henry Tudor's likeness. But I failed to keep him long, more's the pity.'

'Never mind, money is like well-rotted dung, it should be spread about. In truth, I'm Thomas Fleck now, as indeed I was then. What name had you?'

'Folk knew me as Peggy Wath when you strode through here so long ago.'

'Do you keep well, Peggy?'

'An ache and a creak, but well enough. I live with my daughter. Some three years I'm widowed. We manage with my oven, a score of hens and three goats, and there's sometimes bits of field work.'

A horse tossed its head and champed the bit. Rachel dismounted. 'Will you not introduce me to your friend, Thomas?'

Tom felt a flush. 'Ah, I'm given to reverie. Please pardon me. Peggy Wath, meet Rachel, my good wife of twenty-three years.'

Peggy made a slight curtsey. 'A fine, blue day to meet, Mistress Fleck.'

'You will be the girl with the cow and calf. Thomas said you were the first person he met on his adventure. I hope you found him courteous.' Rachel reached for the woman's sun-dark hand.

'Kind and polite, mistress, and that shy he didn't bide long. He rushed off north with a longbow on his back and a little black bitch at his foot. If memory serves me right the creature's head was all bound up in bandage.'

'And me, Father?' Kate dismounted. She held out a hand for a guard to take the reins.

Tom reached for Kate's arm. 'Peggy, this is our daughter, Kate. We travel to London.'

Peggy made another small curtsey. 'London? Where the king bides? Such a great journey for a damsel,' He watched her struggle to make contact with Kate's unfocussed eyes, until she understood.

'I ride a steady gelding, and I've my big dog Bull to spy out the land and keep me safe. Peggy, your pies smell even better than those at home, and I'm hungry.'

He reached into his belt pouch for coins. 'If we take five, will it leave your customers short?'

Peggy's eyes twinkled, and her brown face puckered with crow's feet. 'Indeed no. You'll save my legs. Some days I must tramp miles, and some days I must fetch most of them home. There's no telling with folk. Five pies will be a penny and a farthing, if you please.'

He opened his saddlebag and watched her lower in the brown-crusted pies. Her knuckles were swollen and twisted. 'Your pastry is handsome, and worth all of fourpence to hungry travellers.' He handed her a silver groat. 'If you're ever in want, Peggy, ask for me at Hart village.' He remounted. 'If the way stays dry we sleep at York tomorrow.'

'I've heard York's such a rowdy place where a body must take care — and it has more than its share of ruffians.'

'We'll watch out. And you take care, Peggy. May your days be kind and happy. Perhaps we'll meet again. Farewell.'

'May the saints watch out for you also,' she called after them.

When he twisted in his saddle to give her a salute, he sensed, at the edge of vision, a figure duck from sight behind an ox-cart.

At York they found shelter at the *Rose*, a new-built hostelry and stables beneath the city walls. After supper, their two guards were left to linger over ale, and to chaff serving wenches who squeezed past their armchairs with stacks of greasy platters. The exhausted Kate slumbered in a secure chamber, guarded by her mastiff. Tom and Rachel mounted the steps of the city wall. A stroll along the battlements would ease their saddle cramps. The falling sun gave a pink glow to the pale, fresh-chiselled stone of the inn. Below the old walls, slanted light cut through the branches of orchards bent under the weight of yellow storage apples.

He rested his arms on the lichen crusted, white stones of the wall top, and gazed through the drift of smoke from supper fires, down to the tangle of streets. 'Rachel, such a great city this is. The greatest in the North. Look at the Minster, see how it towers above the huddle of homes, piggeries and workshops. Yon's like a giant in a cabbage field.' He winced at the babel of noise: the bleats of goats, the bellow of a cow, a pair of dogs at each other's throats, the cracked cries of street vendors, the banging of doors, the songs of homeward-bound drunks, and a hunched peddler who called out, 'what d'ye lack?' He turned away from the city of ten thousand people, to face the empty west. In the distance, level acres of river farmland stretched for miles. The sun would soon touch the distant blue fells and sink for the night.

'Yes, a powerful structure. The windows see all ...' She half-choked, covered her mouth with both hands, squeezed her eyes shut and faced the open country.

He touched her trembling shoulders. 'What is it, my love? What have you seen?'

'Let's go. I feel horror. I don't want to linger here. It's to do with that brute.' Her voice shook. She swung around and pointed towards a bulky tower on the far side of the city. 'There is evil!'

'You've seen castles before, Rachel. You've seen the great ones at Durham and Alnwick.'

'They did not freeze my heart. But, York's tower! I feel sick.' She gasped. 'There's a black fear in its stones.'

He folded his arms around her and kissed her cheek. 'This is an ancient place. Much happened, long, long ago. We've ridden hard, my loved lady. We are both faded. Let's to bed.'

She drew the sides of her wimple across her face and linked his arm. They turned their backs on the tower and hurried along the walls to their inn.

While Rachel prepared for bed he went downstairs to seek the innkeeper. The stout man bustled about in the kitchen with two spotty lads. They had blood to the elbows as they skinned, drew, and chopped up rabbits. Tom held his breath against the clammy odour of entrails, though it was not foreign to his nose.

The innkeeper put down his cleaver and wiped red hands on his apron. 'Good evening, sir. Is the *Rose* to your favour?'

Tom nodded. 'I hope the rest of the inns on Ermine Street, between here and London, are as comfortable. You keep a fine house and stables, Master Thorpe.'

'Thank you, Master Fleck. Will you join me in a splash of tawny liquid from France?'

'I will. Though, it must be a brief one — tomorrow we take the highway south.'

John Thorpe put his hands on the shoulders of the lads. 'When you've stripped the conies, set the skins fur to fur like I've taught thee and pack them clean and dry, ready for the curer. Wash the skinned heads and toss them into yon bucket. Likewise, the flesh into this pan. The livers into this bowl and the lights into that'n. The lot can steep in brine overnight. When all's done, get thysel's to bed.'

John Thorpe chose an alcove table away from his other customers. He poured brandywine into pewter goblets. 'Well, sir, good fortune.' He took a swig and eased back into his armchair. 'Perchance I'll be host on your return journey?'

Tom raised his goblet in salute and drank. 'You may well be, Master Thorpe. This is a fine city, with great buildings, though I see the castle is tumbled in parts.'

'Aye, it is. We've asked the king for funds to make repairs, but the city burghers are ignored.' He leaned forward and spoke low, 'York is out of favour at court, we being the city of good King Richard Three. We were never a staunch Tudor town and those in London can bear a grudge.'

'Some folk have long memories,' Tom offered. 'The castle looks a brooding old place. Likely its stones will have tales to tell.'

The innkeeper grunted and lifted the long-necked bottle. 'Another?'

Tom drained his brandy. 'I will — but charge the next one to me.' He leaned forward to breathe in the vapour while the liquid twisted into the pewter cup. 'What age is the castle keep?'

Thorpe drank and wiped his drooped moustaches. 'A good age. Hundreds of years. She makes a mass of stone, and will not be broken. We've learned men in York, with books by the cartload, who reckon Normans built her first, of timber. Either way, she's seen blood aplenty.'

'Sieges and battles, you mean?'

'Nay, not many.' He lowered his voice. 'Butchery of another sort visited that keep a long time ago. Hundreds of Jews died there. Accused of evil practices. Them that didn't kill themselves inside the keep got cut down by the mob when they came out. Black arts or no, a good many slates got wiped free of debt that day, and powerful men grew fatter.'

John Thorpe drew back a chair for Rachel to sit at the breakfast table. 'Good forenoon, Mistress Fleck. Your guards are already well charged for the journey, they've wolfed down porridge and a mound of bacon and fried eggs, but there's plenty left. How do you want your bacon done?'

Rachel smiled at the innkeeper. 'I travel best on more gentle food. Two lightly-boiled eggs and bread, with small ale, is all I need.'

'Ah, same as Master Fleck and the young lady, then.'

Tom waited for Thorpe's heavy tread to fade. 'I like that man. He knows how to balance his words.'

She lowered her voice. 'At future inns we should give our breakfast order before bedtime. A whiff of bacon makes me gag.'

'We'll do that.' He looked at Kate and touched her hand. 'You're pale this morning. How did you sleep?'

'Deep at first, then full of dreams. I'll be glad to leave York; the city smells strange to me. I sense pained old ghosts within the walls.'

'Aye, perhaps you're right.'

Rachel pursed her lips, then breathed deep until her features softened.

They held silence and gazed at their empty trencher boards with eyes half-closed. A pool of quiet surrounded them, with the kitchen's muffled clatter barely sensed at the margins. By the time breakfast arrived, a serene half-smile rested on each relaxed face.

The innkeeper set the bowls of food on the table without a sound. He spoke soft, as though he took part in their communion, 'Here we are now. Eggs light, with warm new bread and best butter. Ale be on the way.'

The innkeeper helped them mount, then took hold of Tom's rein. 'A pedlar just called. He's not given to blather. I trust the man.' He lowered his voice. 'You'd best get south of Yorkshire and East Lincolnshire, hot foot. Folk have risen south of the Humber, with gentlemen's doors smashed at Louth. And there's been killings.' He let his words sink in. 'Our own shire's restless. Agitators. Uproar in Beverley. And they'll march on York. Word is, the whole county will rise.'

Tom grunted. 'They'll have a leader, no doubt.'

'Yes. A one-eyed lawyer called Robert Aske is at their head. He persuades men to swear oaths and join him. If they decline, the common folk break down their doors and carry off their goods.'

'I'd half-expected this. You hear things on the road. Gossip and rumours, mostly.'

'True enough. This time there's talk of new cattle taxes and seizure of monastery land. Churches to be pulled down. No pulpit to be within six miles of another. Parish silver shall be seized by the Crown and replaced with pewter. Gossip and rumour, perhaps. But I've overheard similar when Cromwell's agents stay the night.'

Tom glanced at his two hired guards. They nodded and touched the scabbards of their swords. Rachel paled and stared back at her husband.

'I thank you for the cautions, Master Thorpe. We'll not dawdle on the road.'

9

Humber

Dusk found the travellers at the village of Brough, on the banks of the River Humber, at low tide. Glistening acres spread before them. A tarred jetty of old ship timbers stood above the naked ooze. At the farthest limit of the mud, thousands of waders and ducks sifted and sieved along the margin of the shrunken river. A storm of wildfowl lifted in panic as a goshawk fell amongst them and rose with a shrieking whimbrel in its talons.

There was no sign of a ferryboat, but a crowd of men armed with cudgels and staves loitered at the black door of a whitewashed inn. They gave Tom a quick glare, but avoided the stern eyes of his guards, and instead rested their gaze on his womenfolk.

The heaviest man swaggered up to Tom. 'You intent on crossing to Lincolnshire?'

Tom took his time to look him up and down. He noted the threat in the eyes. 'Why else would I visit a mudflat?'

'You will state your business. I'll take your name and where you're from.'

Tom looked over his shoulder. His hired guards, Percy and Alan Hart, moved closer, spears in hand. He met the man's scowl. 'Who would know my business?'

'You only need know what I do, and that is to guard this bit of the Humber. No man crosses without good cause. You can take the ferry once you've declared yourself and sworn the oath.'

'Oath? What oath might that be?'

The man pulled a folded parchment from his tunic pocket and thrust it at Tom. 'This'n. It's from Robert Aske, the lawyer who leads us. Read, if you can. Then swear on the book, like a Christian. After that's done, you can fare on.'

Tom read the ponderous, flourished script:

Ye shall not enter into this our Pilgrimage of Grace for the common wealth but only for the love ye bear to God's faith and church militant and the maintenance thereof, the preservation of the king's person, his issue, and the purifying of the nobility and to expulse all villein blood and evil counsellors against the common wealth of the same. And that ye shall not enter into our said pilgrimage for no peculiar private profit to no private person but by counsel of the common wealth nor slay nor murder for no envy but in your hearts to put away all fear for the common wealth. And to take before you the cross of Christ and your heart's faith to the restitution of the church and to the suppression of heretics' opinions by the holy content of this book.

He handed back the parchment. 'Have you read this?'

The man looked aside. 'I know what it says.'

'And if I don't care for those sentiments? What then?'

'You get back to where you belong, and pray we don't burn you out of house and home, whoever you are.'

'And the book? What book is mentioned?'

'The Holy Bible of course, man – what else? There's a monk lodged at this inn, he's got the big book for men to lay their hands on.'

'I'll speak to him in my own time, after we've found our chambers and taken rest. Now let us pass.' Tom nodded to his guards. They moved to his side and struck the cobbles with the butts of their ash spears.

The heavy man stepped back. 'Help yourself. High water at dawn and the ferry shall be alongside. Enjoy your meat and bed. Remember what you've been told.'

Tom saw his womenfolk settled in their chamber and sought his guards. He descended the rickety staircase into the ale-room where Alan and Percy Hart sat by the fire with mugs of ale. The stooped innkeeper arranged logs onto the blaze whilst in conversation with the brothers. He straightened, though his spine was still curved, wiped his hands on his apron and gave Tom a quizzical look.

'Good evening, sir. Is all to your liking?'

'Your inn, on the inside, appears decent enough, but I'd not expected to be greeted at the door by ruffians with cudgels.'

The inn-keeper gave a worried glance around the ale room. 'I'm sorry for that, but they've appointed themselves authority. They press men of trade to sign their oath or be ruined. Some gentry flee to escape the oath-taking and hope to keep their names clean in the eyes of the king, but then their houses be looted and spoiled.'

'Have you taken the oath?' Tom watched the anxious eyes and saw the want of sleep.

The man spoke in shaken, muted tones, 'That I have, sir. I don't hold with it, but what's there to do? I fear for what will come from London after all this.' His voice recovered a little of its strength, 'You fare to London, do you, sir?'

From the concealment of a high-backed chair in a dim corner of the room, a man in plain brown leather and linen uncoiled himself. He stretched, and yawned aloud through a full, but grizzled beard.

Barlow rubbed his hands. 'Oh, Master Hill, I didn't know you rested. I'm sorry if my blather woke you up.'

'Nay, inn-keeper, I did not sleep. I dozed and listened to the crackle of the fire and that damned owl on the roof.' He stamped his feet a few times and made his way to the fireplace. Tom noticed the slight drag of one foot.

The innkeeper made a quick bow. 'I've work to do. I must away.' He scurried into the kitchen and closed the door.

Tom stared at the newcomer. Something about him stirred memory; the hard edge to the voice and the slight twist to the nose. As recognition came, the man laid a finger on wide lips and gave a lop-sided grin. A bony hand took Tom's elbow and steered him into the dim corner and a deep chair.

The man took his seat opposite and leaned across, 'I see this mass of whiskers has not fooled you. They must do for the time being, as must the name, but I can't shake off the limp. Mind you, I would now rot alongside my father on Flodden Field if you had not set aside our ill-will and tended my wounds. You could have easily let me die. How do you fare?'

Tom looked into the hooded eyes of Mark Warren. They still held a glint of cunning, but subdued by the years. There had been hatred between this once cruel man and himself. Its origins were years in the past and no longer worthy of effort. 'Life is good. Your young brother Ralph is well wed to my half-sister Mary. They flourish ... Your leg functions still, I see. Any trouble?'

'It aches in cold weather and the foot drags, but the limb gets me about well enough.'

'And the belly gash?'

'No trouble. Your cowherd's stitches left a handsome scar that I show to women who share my bed – it brings out their sympathy. Sad to say my sons cringe at the sight of it. They are as soft as spaniels. Their mother fawns on them. It will be down to me to harden them up.'

Tom relaxed and smiled. 'I find a fortnight with the scythe, or a few acres behind the ox plough, stiffens youngsters well enough.'

'Yes. I hear of your doings; how your bulls are in demand. Your kine are a legend. It's reckoned the fatstock of northern shires is much improved by a dose of your blood. You'll have prospered, no doubt.'

'I'm content.' Tom said. He caught the eye of a serving wench and called for ale.

'And you've a hearty family, I'm told. I last saw Rachel when we crossed the Tyne on our limp back from Flodden. Some years have passed since then; twenty-three as I reckon.'

'Twenty-three it is.' Tom looked into the long face. It held less arrogance than it carried in 1513; some remained, but softened now by age and experience. What brought Mark Warren here?

The ale arrived. In silence they assessed each other. Mark Warren took a swig and wiped his full moustache with the back of his hand. 'You don't say much, but then you never wasted words. You're headed for London. Why's that?'

Tom lifted his tankard. 'To settle a matter.'

'I met your daughter on the stairs. She navigates well for one so afflicted, but why take her on such a journey?'

'To find a skilled physician. We've had enough of quacks with potions and jars of leeches.'

Warren laughed. 'Aye, they're good at bleeding a purse, but not much else. What's the nature of your other business in London?'

Tom slapped the table. 'I settle in a corner with an ale at the far end of Yorkshire and men get inquisitive. Why the interest in my humble doings?'

'Have a care, Tom. You had good cause to distrust me, but that's in the past.' He leaned forward. 'This for your ears only: I'm Thomas Cromwell's agent — Sir Thomas as he's been these last three months. He has the king's confidence and now stands above the nobles in royal esteem. I report to him on matters this far from London. So, you see, I am chartered to investigate all I meet on the highway and even within a man's house. I regularly visit London to report to Cromwell. We will travel together; my two guards shall ride with yours.'

'There's no need.' Tom's stomach knotted. 'I have no dog in your fight. And besides, there's the matter of an oath and a priest I must look into.'

Warren took another drink, set down his tankard, and fixed Tom with a stare. 'Then, you'd best keep a dog in this fight. Cromwell desires to know the mood of your district. I have questions. We travel together, and that's an end to the matter. As for those cudgel-swinging oafs, I'll deal with them on the morrow. You'll take no oath.'

Breakfast came early, an hour before highwater. In the gloom of first light a squat and bluff-fronted ferryboat could be seen rowing its ponderous way across the river.

At the sound of yells outside, Tom set down his porridge spoon. The door burst open and one of his guards appeared. 'Master Fleck! There's a great crowd tramping down the road. They're chanting. They've billhooks and pitchforks. If it's trouble, I doubt we can hold them.'

'How close is the ferry?' Tom stood.

'A furlong. But moving at a crawl.

Mark Warren grabbed his gear. 'Then we had best prepare. Outside everyone!' He threw coins onto the table. 'That will cover us landlord, and there's enough extra to serve out free beer for the lunatics that head this way. Do your best to distract them, and I'll make sure you are remembered when all this is done.' He ran to the back door of the Inn.

'Swear the oath! Swear the oath!' The chants swelled until whiskered red faces crowded the windows, gap-toothed mouths yelling, 'Swear the oath! The travellers clambered from their tables to gather their baggage.

A dozen men with cudgels stamped through the doorway. The leader grasped Tom by his jacket collar and leaned close, 'You've not bothered your arse to see the priest, have you? You don't shift 'til you swear the oath.' Tom backed away from the mix of onion breath and a rotten stomach. Kate's mastiff stalked forward, stiff-legged and snarling. From outside came harsh curses. He heard his guards bawl out commands amid the thwacks of quarterstaff on spear shaft. He landed a fist on the man's nose. The bone crunched. The ruffian staggered back, clutched his face and yelled, 'Grab him! And the women! Take them to the stables. We'll strip them, clout by clout, until he signs. And kill that damned dog, for God's sake!' A cheer sprang from the crowd in the doorway to see the spear sink into Bull's ribs.

Tom looked around the stable from his discomfort amid the dung where they had thrown him trussed. He'd lost a tooth. The horses stamped and snorted. His wife and daughter had been roped to hooks set into the oak frame of the walls. His assailant gave Tom another kick, then with a rag over his bloody nose stared into the eyes of Kate and pulled off her wimple. Her tresses fell about her shoulders.

For the first time Rachel broke her grim silence, 'Harm my daughter and I'll see you die.'

'Is that a fact, Mistress High and Mighty? Try not to be jealous — you'll be next.'

'Leave her. The girl has no sight!' Tom shouted.

'Then she won't blush to see what I'm about to do, will she?' He flung the bloody rag into Tom's face, then put his hands to the hem of Kate's skirts.

From a dark corner, from a pile of loose hay, there came a roar and a bellow. Worn clogs thudded across the dung and clay floor into Tom's vision. There came a sickening soft thud, the ruffian screamed, twisted around, and fell forward with a pitchfork embedded in the small of his back. The owner of the clogs fought like a terrier before he fell, smashed to the ground by cudgels.

Kate called out, 'Wilk, keep still, don't fight them. It is you, isn't it?'

'Aye, it is —' A kick silenced him, but he struggled to his feet when his attackers turned to meet a new threat.

Mark Warren swung a two-handed sword around his head and brought it down on a man's leather-clad shoulder. Both his guards stepped forward to drive spears into two others. The remainder fell back, into the gloom of the stable, and dropped to their knees.

Outside, Mark Warren climbed onto a stone horse-mounting block flanked by his guards in stiff attention. He faced the muttering residue of the mob — the others squatted against the inn walls and happily quaffed from wooden tankards. 'Listen to me! I am

Mark Warren, an official in the employment of your king. If any of you should doubt me, here is the royal seal attached to my orders. Those among you with reading may inspect the king's warrant – are there any?' He held aloft a parchment, its red seal fluttering on a silk ribbon.

Shouts came from the centre of the crowd: 'We don't take orders from the likes of you. Robert Aske is our leader and he'll soon be here.'

'Will he now? Well, I shall be pleased to discuss matters with him, should we meet. In the meantime I advise you to finish your royal ale, and then slip away to your homes. Live in humble quiet whilst your king ponders your petitions. Despite today's misplaced attack on the guards of his messenger, I know him to be an attentive and kindly monarch. Those of you who wish to make royal petition can form a line inside the inn where the priest will record your statement, but be sure to append your signature, or mark, to verify your words. The priest awaits. Better not delay. There is one hour only, I must depart for London on this tide. My ferry waits.'

With horses roped down the centre of a wide and clumsy barge, the travellers tended their wounds as the long sweep-oars rose and fell. Kate, with wet eyes, turned her face to the receding river bank and silently called to the spirit of her slaughtered dog; in her mind she could see his shivering bulk in a ditch where the mob had flung him. Tom drew her close and, in a confusion of thought, ran his tongue around his mouth and poked it into the new gap. He nodded to the shivering Wilk who, stripped to his small clothes, gleamed as Rachel massaged butter into his bruised limbs.

He gathered his focus and took on a stern face: 'You disobeyed me, Wilk. You've slunk behind us. I wondered who flitted behind trees and dodged into ditches when I looked round.'

Kate touched her father's arm. 'Don't be hard on him, Dad. I sensed someone dogged our steps — someone who meant no harm. When I heard those nailed clogs on the stable floor, I knew them for Wilk's.'

'I'm going easy on the lad, Kate. Though I cannot deny that my farmer's wits calculate how deep into the purse I must dig. He's a hero, and they don't come cheap.'

Wilk gave a choked whimper. 'I won't cost much, sir. I've learned to live on next to nowt.'

Tom ruffled Wilk's grubby hair. 'You'll need a good dose of soap and water. And at Lincoln a decent set of clothes if you're to ride into London Town on the pony I shall have to buy you.'

Mark Warren appeared to listen to the talk but keep his own counsel. He opened his pack, took out the roll of petitions and, as Tom watched, threw them into the brown swirls of the river.

10

London

Eight days later, after mysterious diversions to dilapidated inns, a weaver's cottage and a tree-shrouded manor house, insisted upon by Mark Warren, they entered London through Aldersgate under wind-torn skies. Tom Fleck and Mark Warren rode side by side. Mark's two guards cleared the way ahead, scattering throngs of hopeful beggars. Rachel and Kate rode next in line, followed by a wide-eyed Wilk astride a piebald pony. Tom's guards took up the rear, their facial bruises from the fight at the Humber now faded to a blotched and purple-edged yellow. They waited long minutes in a huddle outside Saint Bartholomew's hospital, and rubbed stirrups with other dusty travelers whilst a dead drey-horse was extricated from a sewer ditch and the upturned cart hauled away.

The stench made them gag. Kate had long since drawn her wimple across her face. She opened a fold and gave a small cough. 'Father, that big hospital. Do you think Saint Bartholomew might know about sickness of eyes?'

Tom scratched his beard. 'I don't know, lass. Mark, you know this town, what do you reckon?'

Mark Warren gave a snort. 'That place is a nest of wine-nosed monks, creeping priests, and frauds, whose only medical skill is to bleed you, wave a book, warble Latin round your bed and shrive the daylights out of a man. Go in there and you'll come out with the Bloody Flux.' He coughed and spat. 'If I were sick I'd sooner crawl down a badger set.'

'Oh!' Kate caught her breath. 'Then, do you know of a physician in London with true knowledge?'

Mark's hard face softened a touch. 'There is an easterner. He's maybe an Arab, so I need to check on him. But he's said to be a Christian of some queer sort, and not long here. They say he's brought a new way of healing, and I've had unusual reports. You'll find him on Goose Lane, down by Fleet, if he hasn't been rounded up and accused of sorcery by the bald-pated ones. Name of Gregor Sahakyan.'

'Will you take me to him, Dad?'

Rachel reached for her husband's hand. 'Forgive me, Thomas, I know this city. It's a place of bad air and din, but it was once my home. You will consult him, Kate. We will find this Sahakyan - though a strange name for an Arab. I know and admire the Arabs, their healing arts are not bonded in rock, immovable, like those of the English. If aught can be done, he may know of it. But first we will find the inn where I stayed with Father.'

They passed through the city walls where Newgate street joined Paternoster Row. Picked their way between water carriers, piles of nameless rubbish, and rooting, muck-smeared pigs. Close by, the towering spire and vast church of St Paul's dwarfed the mean structures clustered around its skirts. Beggars crowded the church precincts: disfigured soldiers, withered old women and stick-legged children. Kate felt a feeble tug at the hem of her skirt and the nearness of feminine despair.

'Lady, please. Just a trifle, so my baby can feed.'

Wilk spurred his pony forward and sent the girl sprawling. A thin cry came from the bundle she clutched. Kate slid from her saddle and swept her arms across the ground until she found the trembling girl. She guided her onto her feet. 'I hope your baby is not hurt. You are like me. How long have you had no sight?'

'Near ten years, lady. It was the pocky-pox what did it. Please, we be hungry ...'

Tom yelled a caution to Wilk, then scattered a few farthings among the poised beggars. While they were distracted, Kate dug into her purse. She felt around for the open hand then closed the fingers around a clutch of coins. 'Take these. Hide them in your clothes. And here's an apple and some cheese from the country. May you and your child be well.'

Paternoster Row led them to Ludgate Hill where they passed once more through the city wall. Then across the stink of the River Fleet, through a stretch of mouldered ooze from choked cesspits. And along Fleet Street beneath the carved wooden gaze of Gog and Magog, the giant antique kings. Mark Warren gestured at Whitefriars as they rode past the entrance, 'Those degenerates will be trembling for when Cromwell gets round to them. He'll clear that lot out.' A right turn took them into Chancery Lane at Lincoln's Inn, opposite Temple Bar, where chalk-faced lawyers loitered and gossiped in black robes.

Rachel pointed to a building of yellow Kentish ragstone decorated with patterns of red brick. 'There's our inn, *The Unicorn*. I hope they still have clean rooms. Will you lodge there, Master Warren?'

Mark moved his horse forward. He doffed his broad felt cap to Rachel and then to Kate. 'Alas no. I have my own rooms elsewhere. But first I must seek out my employer. He does not keep such pleasant humour as you ladies. Let's hope he appreciates the reason for my lateness. If I can be of assistance while you are here, Tom has my details. Make sure he keeps his dog on the right side of the fight.' He raised his cap in salute, kneed his mount to a trot, and clattered down Chancery Lane, followed by his guards.

Next day the wind dropped to a whisper. Chancery Lane filled with acrid haze from the coal fires of breakfast time. A confident Rachel led the way on foot to the chambers of her benefactor's lawyer. Grey-bearded and bald, Claude Vaux rose to greet them. He bowed to Rachel and Kate, then shook Tom's hand.

'Welcome to you all. Tis a rarity to have visitors from the far north. I have your letter, Mistress Fleck. It arrived only two days ago — the carrier claimed harassment by mob on the highway between York and Lincoln, and demanded a supplementary fee for his trouble. I hope your own journey proved less arduous. Please be seated.'

Rachel smiled at the lawyer and tried to ignore the nervous tic below his right eye. 'We've had an awkward ten days. We also encountered agitated men. But we met a gentleman on the road who had his own way of calming the mob. They say matters will become worse. Perhaps we should return by sea.'

'Ah, a sea journey has its own hazards. What with the weather and wild men, perhaps worse than the roads. I know how nervous I can be on my rare trips to France and The Low Countries. Home, a coal fire, wine, a book, and a chair that holds me like my mother did, is best for me these days.' He gazed for a while at all three. He lingered on Kate until realisation dawned, and then faced Tom. 'How is the cattle breeding at Hezleden Hall, if I have the right name?'

'It is Crimdon Hall by rights, though Hezleden is close by. The black cattle have done well this year. Some grand young bulls that should fetch buyers from out of the county. Do you have an interest in farming?'

'Only that I envy your life in the fresh air. London makes me cough so.' He smiled at Rachel. 'Now, to deal with the legacy of my client, Alvaro Jurnet. I'll miss him, as will the London poor. A fine old man, a man of wisdom and generous ethics. I understand he was your father's employer. Is that the case?'

Rachel leaned forward a little. 'And his lifelong friend. Like brothers, though master and man.'

'Yes, a most uncommon situation. Alvaro told me stories that I cherish. I wish it could have been such in my own life. I feel the grasp of claws everywhere and few hands extended out of kindness. But enough of that. Forgive me if I should probe with questions. As a lawyer I must be convinced.'

'I understand. You will need to be sure I am who I claim. Please ask as you need.' Rachel leaned back in her seat.

The lawyer dipped a quill. 'Your date and place of birth?'

'The twelfth of April 1491. At Lisbon, a city in Portugal.'

The quill scratched. It caught in the paper and ink scattered with a fan of droplets. He took a knife, trimmed the point and dipped again. 'Lisbon — I journeyed there once; a fine and cultured place. Your religion?'

'My parents were Jewish.'

'As was Alvaro. And yourself? I'm aware there are a few Jews in London, despite the law. Are you a converso? Your husband is born a Christian I assume.' He looked up as Tom shuffled his feet.

'My religious beliefs are my own private matter.' Rachel's voice carried a soft but definite edge.

'And so be mine!' Tom broke in.

The lawyers tic flickered beneath one eye. 'Both responses are boldly delivered and, from what I gleaned from Alvaro, are of a character that should reassure me.' He stroked the goose feather of his quill. 'Have a care in London. There is a hunt on for Lollards, Anabaptists, and similar groups of unusual and modern persuasion.' He gave a furtive smile. 'Now, Rachel Fleck, your father's name and date of birth?'

'Isaac Coronel, born the thirteenth of November, the year 1453, at Lisbon, Portugal.'

'And your mother's, and her maiden name?'

Her melodious voice had an edge to it. 'My mother was Sarah Jurnet, born 1463, Lisbon. She died April 1491, on the day of my birth. Father died twenty-second of August 1513, Alnwick, Northumberland. Cause of death, apoplexy. As a Jew they forbad him the churchyard. He is buried in a woodland glade outside Alnwick, by permission of the owner, the landlord of the White Horse Inn, in the same town.'

She took off her wimple. Silvered black tresses fell across the embroidered scarlet shawl that draped her shoulders. She turned her head and lifted her hair.

'There is this star-shaped birthmark on the nape of my neck, a mark that my uncle, Alvaro Jurnet, would certainly have been shown when I was an infant. Come closer! Do you see it?'

'No need, no need.' The lawyer laid down his quill and unrolled a parchment. He studied the script for half-a-minute, smiled and leaned back. 'I have no more questions. Thank you. You are indeed the person described by my client.'

Flanked by their guards, they departed the lawyer's chambers with five-hundred gold sovereigns concealed about their bodies in small leather bags. Tom, who carried by far the most gold, moved in a more stately manner than was his habit.

The 'Arab' inhabited two rooms in a decrepit house in Goose Lane. Tom surveyed the eroded, smoke-blackened walls and decayed window frames. 'Needs a bit of work before I'd keep hens in it.' But he kept his thoughts to himself and rapped on the door with his quarterstaff. After no response and a second knock, bolts slid back. It creaked open in the hands of a swarthy urchin.

'What for you knock door?' The child grinned and displayed gaps where new teeth protruded.

'We knock to speak with the physician.' Kate smiled at the boy.

He looked quizzically into her unfocussed eyes. 'Wait!' The door closed but stayed ajar enough for them to hear the boy's lilting voice call in a foreign tongue, and a deeper, muffled response.

The door creaked open again. A face the colour of thin peat water looked down on them. The man had brown eyes flecked with green. He stood gaunt inches taller than Tom. 'Who do you seek?' He looked over their heads, up and down the street.

'A healer called Gregor Sahakyan.' Tom repeated the man's gaze up and down the street. 'He's recommended by a friend in the employ of Sir Thomas Cromwell.' Rachel nudged him in the ribs. The 'Arab' noticed.

'Cromwell! He is man of power, yes? Please to come inside.'

Tom motioned to his guards to wait by the door, then led his family inside.

They sat on simple chairs in a whitewashed room and breathed in faint vapours of pine and lavender. A rough cupboard held a few jars and bottles. A padded table stood under the window to the street. Two dirty faces, mucous-nosed, stared through the rippled glass. Sahakyan rose and waved them away. They giggled, stuck out their tongues, and scurried off.

Sahakyan half-closed the shutters and returned to his chair. 'Sorry. Maybe I move from here. Move to another country, even. What you come for? Someone is sick?'

Rachel put an arm around Kate. 'Our daughter, Kate, lost her sight ten years ago when she fell from her pony. We have tried poultices, herb ointments, washed the eyes with herbal liquors, but there's been no change. We hope you have knowledge new to England. Where is your homeland?'

He twirled long fingers in the air. 'Homeland? Who knows? Our people always move. It is enough that I'm Armenian. Head hit by ground? Show me where.' He moved to Kate's side.

'Here.' Kate stroked the back of her skull with a fingertip. 'I didn't bleed, though I was sick. There'd been rain and the field was soft; I shouldn't have galloped. I took to my bed with a headache and the next day could see only a grey light and vague shapes, and the next day nothing at all.'

He placed his chair before Kate, set his hands on her skull, and probed. 'You sometimes see lights in the dark?'

'Yes,' she murmured. 'I see tiny blue and yellow sparkles when I'm excited. They fade away when I'm calm.'

'Keep eyes wide open. I look into them now. You see nothing of me? Anything?'

'Nothing except for little twinkles of blue. But I know what you look like.'

'Say what I look like.'

'You have a long, curved nose.' She stifled a laugh. 'And your ears stick out.'

Sahakyan chuckled. 'True. But you have no sight. How you see my ears?'

Kate gave a small sniff. 'I don't see you with my eyes. But I've pictures in my mind and they tell the truth. I sense things. I usually find my way around. I don't bump into furniture much, and never trees. If I keep calm and let my heart soften, pictures form inside me. Hazy shapes at first, but they grow more solid.'

'Wonderful! Do the mind pictures have colour?'

'Usually they're grey, but other times they have simple colour. I know the yellow of the sand when I sit in the dunes — if I'm calm.'

Sahakyan gazed at Rachel. 'Did you know this?'

'Yes, we have spoken on it. Is it a good sign? Do you know the reason?'

'Nobody understands. I met such in lands of Turk and Persian, but it is rare. It is sight that needs no eye. Kate has special gift.' He ran his palms over her scalp, squeezed with fingertips, probed the nape of her neck, touched her temples and massaged the rear of her skull. 'What happens, Kate?'

'I feel warmth. But there's no change.'

The physician drifted to the window. He opened the shutters and gazed into the smoke haze. He stroked the side of his aquiline nose, gave a soft cough and returned to the visitors. 'How long you stay London?'

Tom answered: 'We have a farm, to the north, ten days travel. We can stay three days more.'

'No time for my work. Problem deep in the head. I cannot see inside and must be guided by heart. I have no treatment except head massage, and I might work months without cure. You could massage for Kate. I teach you method for when at home. If you agree.'

Tom rubbed his chin. 'I've tried my own massage on her, over the years. Folk would say I had healer's hands, but they've maybe lost their power.'

Rachel spoke up. 'We will learn from Doctor Sahakyan. We'll continue his method. It's the least we shall do.' She fixed her dark eyes on the Armenian. 'How long to learn this? Can we begin today?'

'Only one or two hours for you; I sense a family with rare qualities. You will practice on each other and not weary young lady. We begin. Master Fleck have good boney skull; tough like ox. We borrow his ox head to show method. Now start. Please sit straight and still, sir. Keep peaceful. Stay aware of the breath. Listen to my words. First, I show parts of skull. Each part has special doorway to brain. Each door must be opened and massaged in special way.'

11

Ships

Outside the Armenian's shabby door, uproar filled the street. A brawl. Two staggering men threw wild kicks and haphazard punches at each other. A throng of yelling men and women encircled the fighters. Furious dogs dodged between and around their drunken legs. A bucket of foul night-slops splashed across the men. The smaller of the two took the opportunity to drive his boot down his opponent's shin, only to take a bite from a wrinkled mastiff in return. For Tom's party, all hope of a safe route back to the Unicorn Inn faded. Their guards gestured towards a dark side lane, wide enough to allow the passage of four men abreast.

'This should lead to the river, sir. We can make our way back from there.'

Tom grasped Kate and Rachel by the hand. He peered into the mossy ginnel. Tumbledown buildings leaned against each other like a row of drunks. 'Right, Alan, keep an eye out. You lead and Percy takes the rear.'

After a few yards of stepping across nameless waste and the corpse of an emaciated dog, a lank-haired girl emerged from a doorway. Her rouged cheeks contrived to smile at Alan. 'No need to seek further, young soldier. We've a place here with all you'll ever need. Lovely girls and no bugs.'

Alan elbowed her aside. 'Not for me today, bonny lass. Some other time, maybe.'

The alley did a dog-leg to the right, then widened. A cart, with a heavy horse in its shafts, waited outside a corn factor's warehouse. Three men lowered sacks by rope and creaking pulley from a loading door beneath the roof. They whistled and called to Rachel and Kate, 'Now then, honeys! Mind out by the wharf, they don't see many roses down the dock.'

Another dog-leg to the left, and one to the right, spread a vista of the Thames before them as though a stage curtain was pulled aside. Rachel gasped at the forest of masts and spars, stark and stationary against a mid-river canvas of slow white sails. 'Oh, Kate. The ships. I wish you could see all the ships. So many. It reminds me of Lisbon.'

'The smell of tar and salty ropes, Mam. The rumble of barrels. Foreign voices. I do see them. It's magical.'

Tom called a halt. 'Magical maybe, but we'll need to go canny. This is where Alan and Percy could earn their keep.'

Percy laughed. 'Sailors are as scared of a steel spearhead as any footpad. I reckon we head west along the wharf. What say you, Alan?'

Alan looked at Tom, 'That's my sense of it, sir. Shall we get on?'

'We shall, but keep together.' He grasped an arm of Rachel and Kate. 'Don't dawdle, and don't gawp at them Dutchmen's blue breeks.'

Warehouses lined one side of the wharf, interspersed with alehouses and pie shops. Ships groaned and mumbled as their fenders rubbed against the mossy timbers of the quay. Handcarts swayed under bales of wool, pushed and dragged by sweating boys. Porters lugged crates of bottles down a Portuguese gangplank under the eagle-gaze of the tallyman who hovered with knife and marking stick.

They kept a brisk pace, but stopped often to find safe gaps in convoys of oxcarts and pack-ponies. At each halt they would wait in the weak sunlight and dust swirls, pestered by urchins and street pedlars. On the buttress of an ancient ale-house, a cat sat marooned, stared at by a patient, slavering lurcher. From a hole in a rotten board at the foot of a butcher's wall a furred black head peered out. Beady eyes, like tiny grapes, assessed the traffic before the rat scurried across the wharf to board a ship by way of a mooring rope.

'Dad!'

Tom swung round at the familiar and loved voice. In the doorway of the alehouse, clutching a wooden mug, with the arm of a huge African around his shoulders, stood his eldest son. Isaac. He gasped in astonishment.

The next day, Tom Fleck hurried to the wharves to seek out Ben Hood. He found the squat seafarer at table with other ship-masters in a sideways-leaning, timbered inn, with the crude image of a parrot slung above its twisted entrance.

Ben Hood took Tom's arm and led him to a quiet table. He fixed him with a steady gaze from rheumy, red-rimmed eyes. 'You'll come with us then? You'll have to stand your watch though — I'm short-handed. Our mate, that pious grey priest Mister Skerry, has seen fit to sling his hook and move in with a London widow in possession of an ale-house. Most of the galley-slaves we unshackled have vanished into London's muck. You're no seaman, but you're brighter than most and, I'll wager, can lead men.'

'Well, thank you for your trust. But, you could make my eldest into mate.'

'A good lad is Francis. But he's a touch young yet and the old hands might be jealous. Anyway, I need to see more of him before I can sleep easy at sea.'

'Then if I must take a watch, ill-suited though I be, I would have him at my side.'

'And you shall — you're a landsman, after all. Meanwhile, the women shall have my cabin. I'll have carpenters build extra crew shelter. Two more days here, a bit of special cargo, then we sail. I want the ship home afore sunset chases me down. In truth, Tom, I know I'm running out of days. I've the devil's grip in me belly.'

He grasped the ship-master's broad hand. 'We can't have that. I know a good physician here.'

'Never bother. I've already paid out enough silver to the quacksalvers. I've enough to chew on: henbane, hemp, poppy in pig fat, and the like. It all goes down if chased with Low Countries juniper liquor - that Dutch Courage is well named. But I worry over my crew and their rights, should I take bad. I must get my wishes set down.'

'Use my wife's lawyer, he's not far from where we sit. Maybe the time's come for you to come ashore.' Tom spoke low as he rubbed at a knot in the table top.

'I know it. I've been on the world's edges too long. If I'm to be ill, I've a mind to move into that friary atop Hartlepool headland and take my ease; I get on well with the good men at peace there.'

'Then let's hope they're still in peace; the king looks bent on doing away with all such brotherhoods. Their roof might be stripped of lead by now, for all we know.'

Ben glanced around. The ale-house reeked of roast pork and vibrated with song, argument, and the clatter of dice. No-one showed interest in two grey-flecked men in earnest conversation. 'I've heard a lot since we tied up. Henry will ruin this land if he gets his way. He craves money for even more cannon. You should see the workshops he's built at Woolwich and the heaps of metal he's gathered up.'

'If the Friary is no more, where will you bide?'

'I've my simple cottage on the Headland, and a better one at Hart with a good housekeeper. Though, since my purse grew heavy enough for me to enjoy white bread, I'd find a hook to hang my shirt with many a sniffy cousin.'

Tom drained his flagon, set it on the scrubbed beech table, and wiped the bitter froth from his moustache. 'You are welcome to visit at Crimdon Hall. I'd show you a field teeming with green plovers, next to my little hidden wood, called Pyitt's. A sheltered spot, but you can chuck a stone into the sea of a spring tide.'

'Sounds good. I'm partial to a plover egg of an April. But their song and tumbling dance, most of all.' Ben stared into the middle distance.

Tom nodded to his likely new friend. They would enjoy good talk. 'Now, I'd best make speed to the Inn and advise the womenfolk of the benefits of sea air. And I must sell the horses for whatever they will fetch. I'll be back with wife, and a daughter who's blind, two guards, and a boy.' He took the offered hand, measured its strength, and left the alehouse.

Trade ships packed the wharves so tight that they lay alongside each other in rows. The *Encantador* rubbed her black sides against hemp bundles on the thick timbers of a slimy, moss-encrusted wharf. Roped and buffered to the caravel a lean, exotic craft strained against the swollen waters of the river Thames. It was to the latter that Ben Hood guided his passengers across the deck of the caravel. They picked their way through caterpillars of men bent under the weight of cargo.

He paused. 'There she lies, Tom. My new ship. I've called her *"The Saint Mary Boat"* to give her some dignity after her trade as a filthy Barbary corsair.' He whispered in Tom's ear, 'Though I've heard the crew call her *"The Bastard"* on account of the extra work her rig demands.'

Cheerful, profane banter drifted from the open hatches as bale after woollen bale tipped into the gloom of the hold of the *Encantador*. Rachel pulled her wimple across her face - with more sun this could be the wharves of Lisbon.

'*Parada que maldicao!* Stop those curses! *Temos senhoras a borda!* We have ladies aboard!' This yelled into the bowels of the caravel by a gentleman in velvet jacket and breeches. Rachel released Kate's hand in surprise and grabbed her husband's arm.

'Tom! That's Portuguese he shouts!'

A muffled bellow erupted from the hold, 'Stop yer foul-mouthed cursing, you useless bunch of cock-eyed stoats! There's fancy gentlewomen aboard!'

The hold fell into a hush. Then a response from beneath the deck planks that they stood upon: 'Save me a nice-titted one will yer?'

'God's poxes! Get on with yer work, Turd-tooth!'

Tom cleared his throat - the filthy London air had crawled into him. 'I'll wager that's not Portuguese.' Kate gave in to giggles.

The velvet-clad man rushed to their side. 'Senhoras! My apologies for the foul men. I am Henrique Norte, master of *Encantador caravela* - her deck you now cross.'

Rachel set aside the panels of her wimple and smiled into the carefully barbered face. 'Senhor! A gentleman of Portugal! Are you a Norte of the Lisbon house? *Voc um Norte de Lisboa house?* I hope my Portuguese is still bearable.'

'Both are true, Senhora. But my English needs work. You know my family?'

'I'm the daughter of Isaac Coronel. We left Lisbon when I was a child.'

Henrique Norte stroked his goatee beard. 'I recall the Coronels. Trader people. You left, or you fled?'

'We fled. To live as Jews became a crime and a sin.'

'Ah! Those creeping priests! He crossed himself. Such pain they cause with their piety of *el Salvador*. Perhaps some day you will return?'

'Too late for that, sir. I'm wed to farmer Fleck, and am now as English as the rain. My children have flourished like eglantines in northern hedgerows.'

'Two of them Francis and Isaac — yes? Handsome roses, both. Their thorns prick the pirate.' He faced Tom. 'Father of brave eglantines, *saudo a voce!*' He bowed, then took his hand. 'See that vessel? Moored in stream. Hanseatic flag. She is no Hansa. A crew of Arabs and Dutchmen! When you sail, take care.'

The *Encantador* and *The Saint Mary Boat* sailed in company, along with a flotilla of other craft of various rigs. Winter had filled the Thames, and her floodwater bore the fleet without effort to where river and sea mingled in brown and blue confusion. Stark against the gleam of the Medway mudflats, the *Encantador* dipped her pennant in salute and steered east for Northforeland. From there she would tack her way home to Lisbon. The *Saint Mary Boat,* with the wind on her larboard stern quarter, spread her lateen sails and romped into the North Sea chop. Astern of them, other sails ran with the wind, old cogs with weedy hulls lost position as more modern ships gained ground. *The Saint Mary Boat*, with her sleek cedar hull soon led a straggled convoy of vessels bound for the harbours of Northern England.

Ben Hood, wrapped in an oiled cape of sealskin, thick knitted clothes beneath, stood in the stern by the two men on the tiller and watched the shoreline fall away. He grumbled that the ex-corsair's rig of lateen sails obscured the view for'ard. He shouted to the lookout perched on a platform atop the mainmast, 'Owt ahead, Mister African?'

Dayo peered from his place of new freedom, a delightful spot compared to the stench of the oar benches. The sores from his years in slave chains had healed, but the blue weals of them would live on. 'Masts stick up from sea, cap'n.'

'Masts?' Ben Hood lumbered to the mainmast and, with a wince of pain, climbed the rigging. He grabbed the rope that secured Dayo to his pitching station. Clung next to the man, he realised the African smelt different to his beery and herring-breathed Durham crew. Different, but wholesome enough. A touch of musk perhaps. 'Where away?'

'Starboard bow, fine. Is how you speak, cap'n sir?'

'It is. You've keen sight, Dayo. Better than mine. Point for me.'

The African extended a long arm, a great hand on its end, a great black finger thrust to the north. 'There.'

'Ah yes. I have her. She's hull down on the horizon. No canvas. She's hove to. Haunting the dusk. What for, is what I ask.'

'She fishes, maybe. But Hansa rig.' Dayo widened his eyes. 'Maybe Barbary bastards wait. Sit. Bare-arsed, like spider.'

'He'll fail to truss this fly, Dayo. Night's on the way, we'll sneak past him.'

Dayo pointed again, this time to the east. 'Big moon, she come. Soon see everyt'ing.'

Ben Hood cursed. He should have known. The rim of a livid disc broke the quiet horizon. 'You're a canny lad, Dayo. You've a job with me as long as you like.' He yelled below, 'Deck there! Stir yourselves! Clean any muck out of both culverin. I want kegs of powder, scrap metal, chain, and a stack of balls set out. And quick!'

12

The Last Fight

'Helm, two points to starboard. I want him between us and the shore.' Ben Hood looked up at the lateens to observe the effects of his order. Above the sway of canvas early stars fled before the moon. Francis and Isaac Fleck leaned against the tiller, with their father watching. The sails lost some of their belly as they spilled the wind. The hull set up a pitched and twisted motion, and the foresail wandered. 'Come back one point larboard.' The vessel's green canvas tightened. Ben Hood speculated on what effect those outlandish green sails might have on the watchers on Hartlepool headland, should they ever make port.

Francis responded: 'We've lost a bit of way with that move, sir. Tiller doesn't bite so well.'

'Hold your course.' Ben elbowed a path along the narrow deck, through his sparse crew, to climb a few feet up the shrouds of the foremast. He clung there for a while, long enough to stare at the run of the sea, the scattered patches of white water, the moon-flattened shore-line, and the black outline of the two-masted ship that now lay fine on the larboard bow. He winced as he lowered himself to the deck.

Rachel met him, her slim figure buried beneath woollens and cape. 'Can we come on deck, Master Hood? My daughter has a queasiness from the sea.'

He searched the blank eyes of the girl at her side. A touch green round the gills, poor lass. 'Not a good time, Mistress Fleck. In a while there could be a bit of a din, topside. Best for you is the shelter of the cabin. Keep the lass warm and make her swallow some ginger in water.' He saw Tom Fleck watching from the poop and beckoned him down.

'The women are best under cover. I want you and your lads on the poop with your archer's gear. Others will man the helm.' He turned to a shaggy-bearded man, one of the few freed galley slaves still aboard, 'Stefan, you're a Hanseatic gunner, as I recall. If you wish revenge for your shipmates, we may have a cheeky pirate astride our track. I've had the culverins made ready. Will you lay them for me?'

'For you, *capitan*, Stefan lay culverin on all bastards.'

'Good. Get them primed. Fleck's guards will assist and Wilk shall fetch and carry.' Four salt-burnt Hartlepool faces looked on. 'There'll be rope and mast work for you lads. Keep your tackle handy. And Stefan, the lengths of slave chain I had you chop up - stuff them into the culverins. We'll have their guts for garters.'

'Deck there!' shouted Dayo. 'She rigs sails. She moves. She'll cross us.'

The shipmaster hurried to the poop and stood by the new helmsmen, Horsley and Knaggs. 'Hold this course until I tell you otherwise — maybe a half-mile.' He grasped a mizzen rope and adjusted his aching shins to the new deck angle as the night breeze off the land gathered strength. He had his legs well bandaged against knotted veins, the sailor's curse brought on by years flexed on rolling ships.

'Deck there! She dips flag. Two squares. That say Hansa.' The lookout paused. 'Will cross bow ...' A flash of orange cut him short. A light cannon coughed and the sea erupted a hundred yards ahead of the bow.

Ben put a finger to his nose, hawked, then spat over the stern. 'A rogue's salute. He wants us hove-to. He'll speak generous words, then strip us at leisure. The Hansa don't waste time sat around under bare poles. That's the monkey Senhor Norte cautioned on.' He glanced along the deck. His meagre crew stood at stations, by masts and sheets, or knelt by cannon; all eyes were on him. 'Standby for the larboard tack. I want to see his stern. We'll take his wind.' He leaned out, over the swirl of water, and squinted across at the square-rigged vessel on a convergent course. 'Hansa, His Majesty's arse!' he muttered, and waited, and waited ... Then: 'Be you primed, Stefan?'

'Primed both sides, we be,' came the guttural response.

Ben Hood stood erect. 'Standby, then. Larboard, hard!' He watched the square-rigger slip from view to reappear on the starboard bow. 'Helm, that will do. Hold it there.' Under the new course his own sails filled and the sleek hull heeled. Water foamed across the gunnels and around the boots of the crew of the starboard culverin. He stared at the ship, now a mere fifty yards away, and into the mouths of a dozen cannon. A puff of smoke, a cough, and another spout of water rose a few yards ahead.

A yell, thick-vowelled, came across the gap, *'Stoppen! Stoppen!* Or I sink you!'

He sensed the pressure of Stefan's expectant gaze. 'As you counselled, Stefan, when the uproll is right, take the beggar down.'

The Danziger squinted along the barrel, paused for a count of five, and lowered his smouldering match. The flash outlined the drawn faces of those on deck as the culverin gave a belch and leapt backwards against its restraints. Lengths of slave chain raced across the sea to sweep the pirate's deck, rip through her sails and sever her rigging. Canvas and rope fell among her crew and smothered her cannon. From beneath the chaos one gun flashed, boomed, followed by another, and another. A section of plank and ornate guard rail around Ben Hood's poop-deck vanished in a hail of splinters. The dead ball rumbled across the deck and struck a helmsman's boot. On the bows, the crew fled as the foremast of *The Saint Mary Boat* collapsed, under sail, into the sea.

'Axes for'ard! Cut that dog's breakfast free, and quick!'

Horsley gave a shout, 'No steerage! She's dead.' He leaned his gaunt frame into the tiller, nursing crushed toes, as Knaggs and Wilk pulled, both aware of a blood spatter along the beam of oak.

'Leave it! Let her swing as she goes. Stefan, the other culverin, as she bears.' Ben hurried forward with an axe along the deck of his yawing command. As he chopped at ropes with others, he wiped blood from his eyes to discern the figure of a huge man in helmet and breastplate shouting on the opposite poop. A bloody Dutchman, if he ever saw one.

The larboard culverin belched. Across the narrowed gap the pirate's stern was enveloped in a hail of chain that swept its helmsmen into the sea. Ben Hood chopped at the last fouled rope, and looked again. The man in half-armour had vanished.

'We've helm again, skipper!'

He clambered up the poop ladder, thankful he had not been too profit-driven, thankful that he had kept two rowing benches in place. 'Hands below. Oars out! Crawl her round till wind's astern. Mount both culverin starboard side. Stefan, rake his waterline with ball shot as we bear.'

The long cedar hull of the one-time corsair clawed her way past the confusion opposite. At twenty yards, iron balls smashed into the Dutchman's waterline. Tom Fleck and his sons kept up a barrage of arrows, through acrid gunpowder smoke, sufficient to discourage any reply.

At a hundred yards, the listing pirate was too busy at his pumps to be a threat.

At a third of a mile, Ben lowered himself into the foetid gloom of the hold — torch in his fist. The oar sweeps were manned by two ragged Danes, an African, a boy, and — faces plastered with lank and sweat-laden hair — a pair of women. 'You can belay the oars, my people. You did a job of work, that last half-hour.' He eased himself, with a grimace, onto a sweet-smelling bale of Kentish cloth, passed the torch to Rachel, stretched out and closed his eyes.

'He's bleeding. He's white.' Rachel cried and reached for the torn cape. 'We must open his clothes, they're soaked.' She searched his woollens for a way in. A six-inch splinter of bloodied wood had nailed the rough knitting into his side.

Dayo lifted her hands away. 'Leave. Not good to take out yet.'

They watched the grizzled head lift a little. The eyes opened. They shone blue with moisture. 'Aye. Leave her be,' came the murmur. 'It's a lump of scented Atlas cedar from my last command. It's a bit of *The Saint Mary Boat*. You can't have cargo finer than that ... where I'm bound ...' The pale eyes closed as the head sank back.

Along the east coast of England spread a rare, gentle, cloudless December day; a day when, if ashore, a maiden might be troubled by gossamer and must wipe from her cheeks the filaments spun by airborne infant spiders. In low but bright sun, light airs, and on a sea like a rippled and oiled mirror, *The Saint Mary Boat,* with tiller unmanned and lashed, sailed north under two masts, at the pace of a lady who strolled in a garden. She had buried her captain after breakfast that same day. The ocean made one solemn splash as his shrouded body slipped into the North Sea under the weight of sewn-in cannon balls. They watched his journey for two fathoms until the grey canvas faded into green gloom. Rachel and Kate had dried their eyes and now sat together with their thoughts. They relished the exceptional air and the return of pink warmth to their cheeks.

It was time to muster the crew. 'Who shall take command now that we've lost the master?' Tom Fleck addressed a ragged scene of weary men, some bandaged about head and limbs. He eyed the four survivors of the headland crew, all blood relatives, as they gathered in a huddle. His sons stood a little to the side. The four freed galley-slaves leaned against the masts to watch. Despite what they had lived through, he could see this crew had not yet bonded. But those Hartlepool crofters were a peculiar, insular breed. It would take more than a sea fight for them to trust those strangers.

Boots shuffled and Kit Horsley was pushed forward, nursing a limp. He drew his sleeve across his nose. 'As for me, Jack Hart, Boagey and Knaggs, none can stand in for Ben Hood. The best seaman on the east coast, auld Ben was. But we've talked and reckon to serve under you, Master Fleck — till we gets home, that is. We know you for a steady and fair man, and know we'll get our pay, and that you'll make sure Jack Punder's family won't be hungered. You weren't there, but a Barbary crossbow did for him on the Goodwins. If Jack's folk are not looked after, Ben Hood will have no rest.'

'Thank you for your confidence, Kit. But I'm a farmer; I know naught of the sea except that I can have the devil's own job to keep my porridge down.'

'Aye, sir, we've seen you draped over the side.' Horsley turned and scowled when laughter broke out. 'Your lad, Francis, can be mate of the *Mary* till we tie up. He's a sound top on him, and he listens to older heads. What he lacks in sea-time we can make up for.

None of us crofters wants to stand apart in the job ... being such close kin there'd be owermuch cheek.' There were nods and sniffs.

Will Boagey took a pace forward. 'We know Ben found a hoard of coin stashed among the corsair skipper's bits and pieces. "You shall all have your portion," he promised. But then he bought the two culverin. Mebbe it's all spent. But then there's this craft we sail in; we Hartlepool men took her as a prize of war. Will we get our portion of the bounty? That's what we want to know. The lads trust you as a fair gentleman, Captain Fleck.'

Tom Fleck stroked his beard, and tugged at the point. He had not seen himself in this role of shipmaster and lawyer. 'Our late captain might have been a gruff seaman but he cared for those who took ship with him. Even in the midst of pain, he kept you in mind.' He pulled a roll of parchment from his belt bag. 'Captain Hood bade me carry this copy of his wishes and will. He penned it in London before we sailed. It's witnessed by me and by Claude Vaux, the London lawyer of my wife's family. Take your ease on whatever is at hand whilst I read out the gist. I'll set aside the lawyer's blather.'

No-one took their ease. All stood erect and alert.

'My name is Benjamin Hood, shipmaster of the parish of Hart. This is my last testament and will. I was owner and master of The Plenty but lost her on the Goodwin Sands and so I had naught. That same day I salvaged the black caravel, Encantador, but found her master still aboard, and so I had naught. Then I took me a

Barbary pirate as a prize, renamed her The Saint Mary Boat, and my purse bulged again. In those days a man lived as a man should. Now I'm dead, this is how my goods and chattels will be divided and bequeathed:

To my faithful housekeeper Elizabeth Coulson, my cottage at Hart with its furniture, horse, two cows, various swine and poultry. Though this does not govern the bequest, I advise her to now seek out a gentle husband.'

Tom Fleck paused for the snorts and laughter to die away.

'To my numerous cousins and their spawn who, over the years, have offered me damp beds and damper welcomes: At my cottage in Hart there is a broken-down cart, the one with one wheel, they may share that.'

More guffaws. Tom fashioned a stern countenance until quiet returned.

'To Peter Porrit, keeper of the tavern known as the "Pot House", above Sandwell Chare in Hartlepool, the sweepings of my hen house at Hart so that by such means his ale might be improved.'

Shrieks of laughter followed, even from Rachel and Kate, whilst the boy Wilk rolled on the deck, arms wrapped around his sides. Tom waited again.

'*To my dear friend, Friar Gilbert of Hartlepool Friary, my cottage in Middlegate, together with its furniture. It will be a place of refuge for him should the worst come to pass.*

'*And now we shall divide any income from the sale of The Saint Mary Boat and what is in her.*

'*My own fraction of the value of the prize would amount to three eighths. I bequeath that much to begin a school for poor children in Hartlepool, so that their bellies and brains may together be nourished. I hope that Thomas and Rachel Fleck will be trustees.*

'*The mate who signed on The Plenty, Christopher Skerry, gets no fraction. He deserted in London for the charms of a widow in possession of an alehouse. She is a lusty woman. He is well provided for.*

'*The remaining five-eighths will be apportioned thus:*

'*To Anne Punder of Hartlepool, widow of that Jack Punder of my cog The Plenty, killed defending us from corsairs, I bequeath one-eighth.*

'*To the six remaining crewmen who sailed aboard The Plenty, I bequeath three-eighths to be divided equally without favour, so that each man will enjoy a portion of one-sixteenth. That is: William Boagey, Christopher Horsley, Francis Fleck, Isaac Fleck, and Joseph Knaggs. It is Knaggs I thank for his brazen cheek and for keeping a secret smile on my face.*

'*To the freed galley slaves still with me on this day of signing: Stefan Fischer of Danzig, Dayo the African, Axel and Konrad Olafsen, brothers of Denmark, the residue of one-eighth to be shared equally. This is small compensation for their pain at the hands of the Moors.*

'I entrust Thomas Fleck of Crimdon Hall to be my executor. My oaken kist holds sufficient coin to pay my crew's wages. Any coin that remains shall be shared among the above one-time galley slaves in the hope they may find their way home, as all men must. Such is my will.'

13

Light

Her two surviving masts took the cedar-hulled galley close to the low mud cliffs of Norfolk. Tom Fleck and his mongrel crew steered a course that kept sight of land, until they stood off the wide, shallow bay of the Wash. They crossed ragged lines of wool ships, bound for Europe. Deep laden, they had sailed on high tide, out of the harbours of Boston and Lynn. The Boston Stump, that blunt tower of St Botolph's church, in hazy outline on the western horizon, fixed their position.

The Lincolnshire coast came up. The sun went down into marches of sand-dunes, into a haze of yellow and blue-green. A mild southwester drove *The Saint Mary Boat* through the night, toward the great sand arm of Spurn Point, and the start of Yorkshire. With light work and no trace of seasonal North Sea squalls, the crew were cheerful. More sea miles slipped under the keel before the waters of the River Humber came at them at last, in a dun swirl that brought the scents of northern fells, sheep ground and oak wood. Rafts of puffins followed their business on a glittering sea, reluctant to move from the track of the slender ship that sailed through.

For the past two days they met the occasional southbound trader that struggled against head winds. Some passed on a broad tack, and close enough to exchange news. It followed a pattern:

'What news of the rising?' Tom Fleck yelled across the iron-blue water.

'The Duke o' Norfolk met the twenty-thousand at Doncaster to talk truce. It's mebbe all over,' came the response from the latest Tyne collier, deep-laden for the Thames.

'Any trouble?'

'Not much. Just a score of burnt houses and some gentry with bruises. Thousands set off home. The king makes promises.'

'Will he keep them?'

'Who knows! Some captains o' the Pilgrimage think not, and slip out of England by any means. We shall see.'

'Fair winds to you.'

'And to you.'

Three times a day, Kate sat in silence whilst her parents massaged her head in the manner taught by the Armenian. Rachel and Tom, by common consent, declined to ask if there had been a change. After the treatment, Kate, wrapped in a cape, would feel her way for'ard, and kneel, head tilted toward a point a few yards ahead of the bow wave. With a crewman posted nearby, she would remain like that until the spray became too much.

This morning, Dayo was posted. He felt kinship with the girl and knelt beside her to follow the line of her blind stare. Ahead of the bows the usual pod of dolphins, adults and young, broke surface, leapt and dived, again and again. 'Eight eja fish today, Miss Kate. Yesterday only four.'

'Yes, Dayo, I know. This is a new clan. Yesterday's little dolphin family went home. They can only stay for a while.'

'How you tell? Eja fish look all same to me.'

Kate did not respond, but he watched her smile grow.

He asked again, 'How you tell, Miss?'

She turned to him. The low sun brought a violet cast to her unfocussed blue eyes. 'I listen to their talk. It's not human. But I feel the words.'

'Where you feel words?'

'Inside.' She touched her heart.

'You special. What eja fish say?

'They laugh and tell how they live in joy.'

'Ah, dayo! That my name. Yoruba mother call me Dayo. It mean, 'Joy Comes'.'

'Then maybe you can hear the dolphins, the eja fish. Listen to them, they will go soon, back into the big river away to our left.'

Dayo leaned over the bow. A six-foot dolphin broke surface and, with a miniature of herself as though suspended beneath, leapt in a dripping arc to plunge again. Foam lashed his African features. He wiped the spray from his short beard of tight curls, and chuckled. 'They whistle like little people in forest, then go click, click, click.'

'You have little people in your forest. Are they fairies?'

'Not know fairies. Little men teach forest magic to Yoruba. If Yoruba sick, little people make better.'

'They sound like fairies. Dayo, can I ask what you did before the Moors took you?'

'Help mother work with herbs. Then, when strong, make metal alongside father. Make big fire, make big wind go through. Make bronze heads for chiefs. Moors take Dayo far away. They want metal secret, but Dayo hate them, break heads, so get chained to oar in galley. Years go by. Hurt bad. Dayo lonely. Make friends of man next to me, but he always die. Lonely again.'

She searched and found his hand. 'I'm sorry you were lonely and are so far from home. I hope someday you can return to your people.'

'Home burned by Moors. People run away. If Dayo go back, he take army with him. Isaac brother now. Stay alongside brother.'

'What did your mother do with the herbs? Did she heal people like the little people did?'

'Yes, she see what they did with herbs and with hands on head. Blind Yoruba, who live on swamp river, come to mother. She with magic hands. Some run home without stick.'

There was silence. Then: 'I wish I could go to her.'

'She good with blind man from swamp river. Blind from worm, she say. Miss get eye sick another way, I think.'

'I fell from my pony. When I stood up, the light had gone.' She pressed long fingers against her scalp, and massaged.

'Dayo watch Kate's father and mother do that. Does light come back?'

Long moments passed, they listened to the slap of water on the hull and to the harsh cries of a mob of terns that dived for sprats. 'I've not told them yet, but sometimes I see white sparkles. Sparkles like I remember would dot the sea on a calm and sunny day. But I've not told them. It might be naught. The sparkles fade after a while.'

'Will Kate let Dayo touch head?' Before she could respond, the African's fingers probed her skull. 'Kate says if it hurt, yes?' The fingers roamed around until they settled on one small area. They paused, pressed, paused and pressed again, then squeezed and stretched the scalp. 'What Kate feel now?'

'I feel as if in a trance. My head feels hot and full. I'm afraid. But don't stop. Oh!' The strong finger tips rotated, pressed and rotated again. They gave one final press and then released.

'Dayo stop now. Enough for Kate today.'

'Oh, Dayo, I might have seen dolphin shapes, with sparkles around them.' Her arms stretched towards the bows. The fingers extended and cupped as though to capture an elusive sprite. 'Dayo, the dolphins were silver flashes and the sparkles like drops of fire. But there's nothing now except little bursts of light. How did you know what to do?'

'Mother have magic hands. Dayo learn same. Kate now go, lie down, close eyes. If Kate father say yes, we do again, after sleep.'

'The dolphins! Danger comes. They're afraid. They rush for deeper water.'

Dayo scanned the sea and saw nothing until he looked astern. The pod raced towards the southeast. In all directions, the usual flotillas of seabirds had abandoned fishing and were in flight. Puffins and guillemots now streamed in long lines after the dolphins. Overhead, gannets and fulmars moved in wide circles. 'Then we go too,' he murmured.

Kate picked her way against the slow pitch of the deck towards the stern cabin. Davo stayed a pace behind, with arms outstretched ready to grasp should she slip. Her father and her brother Isaac, and those of the crew on deck, watched in silence.

'Deck there! Have a care!' The yell came from Will Boagey high in the mainmast rigging. 'Off starboard bow. A big'un coming. Looks nasty. A mile off!'

Francis Fleck grasped the rigging, then climbed. His father followed. Once clear of the green lateen sail, they paused, and stared to the north-east. Francis tightened his grip. 'My god! It's the height of a mast, and makes for us. Deck there! Crew standby.' They scrambled back to the deck, past hesitant sails that swung and flapped. 'Close that hatch, then everyone, except the helm, take cover and make yourselves fast. Isaac, get Rachel and Kate to the cabin!' Francis and his father ran to join the two men at the stern.

With scattered veils of cloud in the sky, and in light airs, with the sea a mere glassy heave, four men tightened their grip on the tiller beam. A long, pillow-like hummock of water defined the horizon. The wave grew in height and menace as it approached. In the distance a fishing coble, with its simple sail and two men, was overwhelmed. Despite the uncertain breeze, the galley gathered speed sideways as if some force sucked at the hull.

The Danes, Axel and Konrad Olafsen, joined them at the tiller and heaved on the beam. 'Swing her. Steer into it!' They shouted together across the whine of a sudden blast of wind.

'What is it? What comes?' Tom Fleck, his expertise in archery and husbandry of heavy cattle, now of no account, knew the despair of the useless.

Axel, eyes bulging, and his yellow beard flared around his chin, gave him a hard stare. '*Soskaelv, kaptajn*. Seashake! Here is too shallow. Big wave come. *Flodbolgen*! Same when Norway cliff fall into sea - harbours empty, then sea come back and Jutland drown. All men must rope to masts.'

The wind grew, the rigging hissed, and the two remaining masts groaned as the galley clawed onto her new course across a sea laced by blown spume. With her bows now pointed toward distant deep water and away from the shallow Yorkshire coast, and with the soft, earthen cliffs of Holderness a bare mile astern, the cedar galley and her people waited to be drowned. Tom glanced at the shore. Now was the time of high water, the sea should be chucking itself at those ramparts, yet an expanse of sand streaked with bands of brown clay made a great skirt. And the beach widened. 'Axel. The tide is running out. 'Tis unnatural. What do we do?'

'Meet *flodbolgen* with bows. Too late for —.' The Dane's voice was obliterated by rasps beneath the hull. The tiller throbbed in their hands and the deck under their feet set up a vibration. *The Saint Mary Boat* groaned her way across sandbars, pulled by a retreating sea.

The wave grew in height, smooth and swollen. It was invincible — like echelons of pikes. Tom Fleck stared wide-eyed and knew terror for the first time in the twenty-three years since Flodden, when that forest of Scottish pikes descended the slopes of Branxton Hill and he quailed as he fumbled with his longbow, his dog whining between his spread feet. A hundred yards to the left it climbed, curled and broke. He gasped as the bows knifed into the slope of the wave front and disappeared. The hull shuddered beneath the weight of tons of cold sea. With slack sails, she halted as though out of breath, then pitched upwards to the cries of her people and the clatter of loose tackle. His knuckles whitened as he watched a culverin tumble from its cradle. The iron canon rolled towards the stern, snagged on ropes, severed them, spun around and made men leap for the shrouds. 'Keep the tiller!' he yelled. He trembled in his bowels as she climbed with a foot of water sliding off her deck.

She found the wind again, perched on the crest, paused as though to breathe and, with groans from her planks, plunged downwards. The crew tensed for the crash that would come when the hull touched bottom. But the sea bed fell away, and with faint scrapes the galley slithered her way across sand and gravel into deeper water. Astern, the wave slammed into the base of the cliff and acres of sheep land fell to the beach. Holderness boiled white with foam and glistened with glacial clay not seen for twenty thousand years.

'Another! Another comes!' The bellow came from Will Boagey, roped high up the mainmast. 'Half a mile she comes!'

The six men on the tiller were now five. Axel, the Dane, lay crumpled on the deck one arm around a rope and the other strangely limp. He called out, 'Steer into it, *kaptajn*. More will come. Steer into them.'

Tom Fleck shouted along the deck, 'Dayo! Dayo, where are you? Get down here and look after Axel.'

'Dayo come.' Dayo's head emerged from a pile of loose tarpaulin snagged around the foot of the mizzen mast.

'Deck there!' Tom shouted again. 'The starboard culverin broke loose. Have we lost it?'

'No, Captain. She's rammed into the cabin, snout first.'

'The cabin? The women are inside! Pull it free.'

'Too late. Here comes the next one ...' Francis and the haggard tiller men put their weight on the oak beam.

More of Flodden replayed itself through Tom's mind as he clung to the tiller and waited. The waves of massed Scottish pike-men leaping his prone body. That fearsome lochabar axe, and the hate in the face of the giant that swung it. A flash of thought: If we survive this I'll have learned summat of the sea. He grinned, then brayed out a laugh. 'Sod this for a game of soldiers,' he roared as the bows thudded into the second wave and the galley was buried again. But she rose up like a great northern diver with a fish in her bill, and climbed. A snapped rope lashed his face. Blinding pain and blood in his eyes. Her steep plunge down the far side released the culverin from the stove-in cabin. It set off on a thunderous roll towards the bows where it ripped away the guard rails and fell into the sea. Under a darkened sky the lateens filled with the wind and rain of a chasing squall and drove *The Saint Mary Boat* towards the next wave. She mounted it like a solan goose, leaned with ease, and sped onwards.

Francis Fleck, at the tiller, craned his neck and yelled. 'Will Boagey! You still up there?'

'I am that, Mister Mate. Though I be well bruised.'

'What's ahead? Owt else coming?'

'Nowt in sight. A bit of a chop getting up, but no big'uns. That was a tale to tell the bairns. Can I come down now?'

'Stay there 'til I send relief. Won't be long.' He turned to his father, but he was gone. Tom Fleck was at the cabin front with his son, Isaac, where they wrenched free the buckled and splintered timbers. Wilk stood by and cleared wreckage from around their boots.

Inside the cabin Tom sobbed at the sight of his wife and daughter, bodies wrapped together by torn and blood-stained arms. Sea-water swilled across them at each pitch and roll of the hull. As he bent to their limp forms, Rachel opened her eyes. They were glazed. 'Is it finished now?' she murmured.

'It's finished. You are safe.' A lump like a swallowed apple formed in his throat. It was love. He took one grazed arm. 'Now let go of Kate so I might lift you free, then I will lift her.' He looked over his shoulder. 'Isaac, have Wilk fetch blankets from the hold, cut up a bale of that London cloth if you have to, and shout Knaggs to stoke the stove. We want hot broth, and quick.'

He lifted the weight of her, heavy with saturated gown and cape. The silver-streaked black hair clung to her features like winter beached kelp after high tide. Her hand touched his cheek. 'Look to Kate. She still breathes. I lay on top of her when the wave came.'

'I can see that you did, my brave wife. Stay quiet, now. Isaac is here to help.' He passed her through the ruptured doorway of the cabin and into the arms of her second son.

Kate's breast rose and fell, but she seemed to have no wits. He rubbed her hands, then slapped her cheeks. 'Kate. Wake up now, wake up. It's all over, and we go home.'

'Go home? I want to go home,' she muttered through lips salted white. Her eyes opened. She reached out, touched his face, then looked at her fingers. 'Blood. Oh, father. Your poor forehead is covered in blood. I can see it. I can truly see it.'

14

Harbour

The vast white cliffs of Flamborough reared out of the haze and flushed pink as sunrise burned through a dawn sea fret. Red-eyed, Rachel and Kate knelt by corpses and arranged wrappings on the deck of the galley. Mottled faces stared back. Three fishermen stiffened, part covered by tarpaulins; men found roped to an upturned coble and gathered from the sea. The knitted patterns on their woollen jerkins said they came from Filey. The crew of *The Saint Mary Boat* lifted the drowned, one by one, and passed them over the rails into the care of a local fishing boat that had ventured out for survivors of the giant wave.

An exhausted face, encircled by white whiskers, looked up from the Filey coble. 'The monster came yesterday and took folk away. We thank you for these three. One of them looks to be my sister's lad, bless him.'

'What numbers are lost?' Tom asked.

'A dozen coblemen set out and have not come back. Some women bait diggers were swept off the beach and are gone. Those not tangled in kelp will have drifted south on the longshore current, whether they live or no. All we've found so far is men from the north

- Scarborough pattern on their woollens. Their women will likely be here tomorrow to search for their own knitting. Scarborough will haul out the drowned of Robin Hood's Bay. And Bay will fetch ashore the Whitby men. Any not found should wash up on Spurn Point. This coast might have lost a generation. I've seen nowt like it.'

'We'll keep an eye out for others,' Tom said.

'The priests have come running across the hills. Folk ask of them, "Why us?" God must be well vexed, even though it's not us who harmed His church. 'Tis the king who's stripped the monasteries.' The corners of the faded blue eyes showed the start of tears.

Tom stood back as the last corpse was lowered into the coble. 'It's nowt to do with God, king or priest. We've Danes aboard and they reckon it's from some giant cliff fall. Axel says half a mountain can tumble into the Norway fjords. He's worried about his own village in Jutland. It's got less freeboard than here.'

'Aye, I do recall that low place. Nowt but sand.' The white whiskers twitched. 'Even so, there's many a Filey goodwife plodging about amid her treasures today.'

'Do you head home now?' Tom asked.

'Nay, we've come this far, so we'll take a look close inshore and among the rocks. We want them out afore the crabs take hold. It's a bit early though; most of the perished will not rise for a day or two. We'll cast off and wish you well.' Oars pushed the clinker-built coble away from the galley. She hoisted her threadbare scrap of square sail and ragged morsel of jib, then steered for the coast.

Tom watched them depart and wondered at the brave poverty. It was a topsy-turvy world. Such a struggle to live. Hard knocks and cold drownings, and all the while velvet-clad folk in London's great halls dined on swan.

They passed black cliffs in moonlight. The watch on deck were numbed by a knife-edged wind from the north-east that raised a disorganised chop. It pressed them against the coast and they needed oars to fight for sea-room. The lateen sails emptied and filled as they made tack after tack. Axel, on a rowing bench, alongside Isaac Fleck and Dayo, wiped sweat from his neck as the bows hit another lump of green. '*Vesterhavet!*'

'What's that, Axel?' Isaac sucked his palm where a blister had lifted beneath his callouses.

'*Vesterhavet*. North Sea, you call it. Axel near home. Not smell this sea for two years.' They leaned back together and pulled in harmony with three other oar-benches.

'Dayo never so cold. Sweat cold. But happy. Happy our Kate see again.'

At the stern Kate sat wrapped in a length of expensive red London cloth borrowed from the cargo. She gazed at the cliff as a full moon emerged from a veil of cloud to hang above the black outline of a great building. A few lights twinkled around the base. 'What's that place on the cliff top?'

Tom Fleck leaned into the tiller with three others as a wave pushed the galley's head towards the coast. 'Will Boagey, here, tells me it's Whitby Abbey. He's got a few cousins in the town.' The bows swung and recovered the course. Wilk climbed the short ladder and took his place. Tom edged across the pitching deck to squat beside his daughter. 'I've never been there, but I recollect the abbot of the place sent a hundred or so to Flodden. I spoke to some of them on the march back.' A rush of frigid air hit the vessel and it leaned. 'Kate, you should be in the cabin and not out in this night wind.'

'This bright red cloth is warm and thick. No wind gets through it. I'll make it into a shawl when we reach home. Heads will turn in Hartlepool.'

'Aye they will, lass. Heads will turn, right enough. Have you not heard of the Sumptuary Laws? Our class of folk are denied that colour. It's reserved for nobles. Russet is the nearest to what we can wear. There's russet cloth in the cargo. You shall have some; though it's not as fine as yon.'

'But you're a yeoman, Dad. And you fought for the king. Why can't we wear red?'

'Nobles make the laws. They don't want men with broken nails to get above themselves. That's the way it is. For now, anyway.'

Caught by the sky's cold light, Kate's eyes flashed. 'Then the nobles have not the wits of a dog whelk.'

Wilk had sharp ears. He gave a boy's broken-voiced roar. 'That's a good'un! Though I hear Lord Clifford's eldest lad, the fat one at the big house, can sometimes outsmart a herring ... But only if it's been kippered.'

Tom's involuntary snort of laughter was lost amid the sniggers and guffaws from the helm. He swallowed a couple of times. 'That's enough now. Bobbing about in the North Sea we might be well out of earshot of any great house, but I fear you'll let slip when you're ashore and wind up in the stocks — or worse.' He leaned closer to his daughter. 'How are your eyes? I hope you take care of them. Do they see the rags of cloud and the man in the moon with his round face?'

'I see it much like I remember as a child, Dad. But tonight there is no man. I see a dog in the Moon.'

'Just a dog? Not the poor man banished there for gathering sticks of firewood on the Sabbath? Or Jacob of the Israelites, as your mam would have it?'

'I used to see his sad face, long ago. Some nights my mind saw a hare. Tonight there's a dog in the Moon. And he's running.'

A watery dawn sun, with a line of gannets silhouetted, climbed out of a rippled sea to the east and cast a pink glow onto the straw-coloured cliffs of the headland. The Norman cathedral church of St. Hilda emerged from thin mist. From its high place it dominated the huddled cottages of crofting fisher folk, but not the tall houses of merchant gentlemen gathered close to the church; close to God and remote from the fevered lanes of the Croft. A half mile ahead of *The Saint Mary Boat* a Hanseatic trading ship with bare masts crawled toward the inner harbour under the tow of a flotilla of rowing cobles. Squeals drifted seawards from twin towers as the chain that guarded Hartlepool was cranked and lowered into the water so that the foreign merchant vessel could enter. The squeals subsided as men pasted ox fat onto dry iron cogs. The crew and passengers of *The Saint Mary Boat* lined her rails.

Those of the town joked and chattered with relief now that their hazards were done. The freed galley slaves kept their own counsel, thoughtful on how they would be received. Dayo, the African, stood by Isaac Fleck, his *new brother*. Isaac sensed concern and placed a reassuring arm around the bulky shoulders.

Francis Fleck raised his eyebrows to his father. Tom Fleck responded, 'A difficult bit here. You are the seaman, lad. Take us in.'

Francis cupped his hands around his mouth, 'Masthead man to the deck. Sail crew, lower and stow all canvas neatly, folk ashore are watching. Oarsmen, to the benches and take her in; just a bit more effort, if you please.' He smiled to see his crew scramble to their stations. A cannon belched from the town wall. The shot splashed fifty yards ahead of the galley's bow. Francis turned to his father, 'Not the welcome I'd hoped for.'

Tom Fleck pointed, 'There's a coble coming out. Men in Tudor colours. We'd best tread water for a bit.'

Francis strode to the hatch. 'Easy on the oars. Just keep her from drifting.'

The big coble drew closer. Five bearded men in knitted woollens manned the oars. Bow and stern were crammed with green-and-white uniformed soldiers encumbered by spear and arquebus. They drew within hailing distance, and hove to. 'What ship? Where from?' The yell came from a breast-plated man whose arms were wrapped around the single short mast.

'*The Saint Mary Boat,* out of London, late under command of Ben Hood, shipmaster of this town.'

'You look like a pirate,' came the reply.

'She was indeed a pirate. Ben Hood took her, off the Goodwin Sands.'

'I would speak with Ben Hood.'

'Killed by the Dutch a few days back. I'm in charge. Tom Fleck of Crimdon Hall.'

The coble pulled closer until a rower shouted, 'Tom Fleck it is! He goes to London on a horse and comes home in a galley rigged like a dog's breakfast. I see Will Boagey on the bow, and there's Knaggs with his ugly mush.'

Knaggs threw a fish head at the coble. It fell short. 'You watch your lip, Cush Coulson. Any barnacled arse looks better than your auld face.'

The officer who clung to the coble's mast bellowed, 'That's enough! We come alongside and make inspection.'

The galley, her deck now sprinkled with soldiers who carried on a furtive trade for London trinkets with her crew, eased into the inner harbour under oars. Watched by a press of barefoot children, women in shawls and men in patterned woollens, and to the barking of dogs, she slid with ease alongside the wharf, astern of the Hansa ship, and was secured fore-and-aft. Tom Fleck jumped ashore and took the arm of Dolly Punder. He led her beyond the crowd. She focussed her faded blue eyes onto his. 'Where's the *Plenty*? My Jack. What's happened to him?'

Before Tom could respond, Francis appeared at his side. 'The grand old *Plenty* is lost on the Goodwins, Dolly. Your son stood at my side when we fought off the Barbary pirate. He was a fine, brave man. We buried Jack at sea, in a manner fit for the proper sailor he was. We have his wages, and a good bit more besides; Jack's wife and bairns will be safe.'

With a piebald trio of hired pack ponies, loaded with the essentials and ephemera of their journey to London, and a length of London red cloth pressed on Kate by the crew of the galley, they climbed the ridge of the headland and turned towards home. Tom called a halt at the gate of the Friary. The drinking trough maintained by the friars for the comfort of travellers and animals, was dry except for an inch of green scum in which an unfortunate beetle, a devil's coach horse, struggled. He dipped a finger and lifted the drowning creature to safety, then stared through the gate.

The Friary roof had gone. Labourers were rolling up strips of beaten lead. Three soldiers sat on piles of masonry, casting dice. In Friar Gilbert's herb garden, a billy goat pulled at trampled plants. Tom called to a labourer who trundled a barrowload of rotted dung toward the gate, 'Where's Friar Gilbert?'

'Gone to Durham, with the others, to plead with the bishop. Been gone a week.' Tom recognised the man as local.

'A long way at his age. How is he?'

'Sprightly enough, but downcast. They went out on a dozen grey donkeys sent by the Bishop.'

'Thank you, for that. Who takes down the friary?'

'A noble from Guisborough way. A fancy name I don't recall. Bought the place from the king, it's said. This auld muck is going free, so I'll scatter it on me kale bed. A bad business, but what can we do?'

'These are times of greed,' Tom answered. 'Keep close to your own hearth and what you value most.' He glanced at the soldiers intent upon their dice, and motioned his party onwards.

By the tumbled stones of Saint Helen's chapel, neglected for a generation, he paused to take in the landscape from that high ground. To the south, against a duck-egg-blue sky, the toothed hill of Roseberry wore a shoulder wrap of early snow, prominent above Cleveland and his youth. Moorland for miles, he pondered. A sea of heather and ling, and red grouse that shouted, 'Go Back! Go Back!' Summer curlews that throbbed. Skylarks like dots in heaven, bubbling with the joy of it all. But winter now, and most would be picking about for a living by the seashore. Rachel's thoughts were on him. He looked at his wife and noted her half-smile. After twenty-three years those dark eyes could still bring a tremble. 'Rachel, I'll be home a bit after you. I'm going by the dunes; I want to check on the heifers that run there. You take the low route. Francis can lead you in just as well as I might.'

When he reached the dune crest he looked back. Wilk was striding out, pony ropes in hand; the adventure had brought on the first signs of manhood - no more cracked warble in his voice. Isaac trailed behind, pointing out things to his new brother - what would become of Mister Dayo? Children's eyes were wide with wonder when the big African had jumped onto the quayside. He pressed on, into a sandy hollow where the arched marram grass scored graceful arcs into the silky sand.

Kate watched her father vanish from the crest. 'I'm going the way of the dunes too. I'll catch him up. See you all at home.' She hitched up her skirt hems and ran across the sheep pasture into the wind-swept marram grass.

Dayo watched her go. Her lithe strides reminded him of the desert gazelles he'd seen when, chained by the neck to fellow captives, he'd been marched across the great sand-sea by the Arabs. He shook his head to break a memory of the lash. He saw instead, his betrothed, tall and lean, mystical like Kate. She did not survive. For him, she lived again in that English girl who darted into the sand dunes.

Tom Fleck strolled up to the black bull. The animal lifted his head from pulling at clumps of fog grass on the most ancient dune and, with a soft snort, took a pace forward. Tom stroked the white blaze on the great forehead. 'Now then, Satan auld lad. How are you keeping? Have you been doing your job with the ladies? Plenty of fresh air here for thee; not like in London where I've been. Dust and dung, folk with scabs, folk in silk. I'll not go there again, if I can help it.' He turned to see Kate sledging down a sand slope on her backside. She reached the bottom and sprinted towards him.

'Dad! Wait for me.' Her cheeks were pink with exertion. Best of all, the excited sparkle in her eyes. 'Let's go home by the mound and the place I used to sit with my dog. I've touched it, smelt it, listened to it, and even tasted it. I want to know its colours.'

The summit of the burial mound, crowned by the familiar stunted hawthorn, rose above the undulations of blue-green marram. It rode like a ship at sea. From out of the hissing grass a head appeared. A broad brown mastiff head. The dog gave a long wolf howl and bounded towards them, barking.

Kate skipped forward. 'I knew it. He found his way home. I saw him in the moon. It's Bull!'

The End

Story Background and Historical Note

This story follows the struggles of a fictional farm labourer in North-East England. The series began with the novel, 'Tom Fleck', in which we followed Tom's adventures, loves, and troubles in the year 1513, the year of the Battle of Flodden. The present book re-enters his life twenty-three years later in 1536, at the start of the dissolution of the monasteries and the subsequent rebellion known as 'The Pilgrimage of Grace'. Tom is on a journey with his wife and blind daughter and must travel through the chaos.

I've used the names of two early ships whose existence is recorded in the seaport of Hartlepool: 'The Plenty' and 'The Saint Mary Boat.'
The names of fictional natives of Hartlepool, and of its seafarers, are derived from the old fishing families of the Durham coast as recorded in local parish registers.

In Tom Fleck's musings on his walk to market in chapter one, his thoughts on the 'giant warrior from Gotland' allude to theories that Hartlepool headland (anciently: Heortnesse) and the nearby village of Hart (Heorot) are the setting of the early English saga of Beowulf. Archaeologists in Hart village found a huge

Danish hall. Some speculate the place to be Heorot, the mead hall defended by Beowulf from Grendel's attacks. The sea caves at nearby Blackhall Rocks, and the tidal saltmarsh that was the Slake (before it disappeared beneath Victorian docklands) gives the theory some support.

Trouble came to northern England in 1536. Many detested how Henry VIII had cast off his wife, Catherine of Aragon. The execution of her fleeting successor, Anne Boleyn in 1536, on bogus charges of adultery and treason, further undermined the king's prestige.

It became a year of protest in Yorkshire; protest against the king's severance of England's ties with the Church of Rome, his suppression of monasteries, and the policies of his 'base born' chief minister, Thomas Cromwell. The outcome was 'The Pilgrimage of Grace' and the allied 'Lincolnshire Rising'.

Robert Aske led the Yorkshire insurgents. Aske was a barrister and son of Sir Robert Aske of Aughton, near Selby. In 1536, Aske attracted a band of 9,000 followers, who marched on York. They returned expelled nuns and monks to their houses, and Catholic observances resumed.

The rising obliged Thomas Howard, Duke of Norfolk and royal negotiator, to parley with the rebels near Doncaster, where Aske had assembled almost forty thousand men. Norfolk commanded only thirteen thousand.

Norfolk offered a general pardon from the king, and a reprieve for the abbeys, pending a meeting of parliament He persuaded Aske to have faith in the king's promises. Aske dismissed his followers and all returned home.

Henry VIII's revenge came the following year when, after another failed rising, (under Sir Francis Bigod), Norfolk embarked on over two-hundred executions of nobles, gentlemen, abbots and priests. Among the executed were Bigod and Aske (who appear in this story). Tragically for Yorkshire, Sir John Bulmer, son of the hero of Flodden, was hung, drawn and quartered in London at Tyburn. His mistress, Margaret Cheyney, illegitimate daughter of the Duke of Buckingham, was burnt at the stake at Smithfield. Margaret, mother of a three-month son, was the only woman to pay the ultimate price. Her cruel punishment was intended to be an example to others.

Printed in Poland
by Amazon Fulfillment
Poland Sp. z o.o., Wrocław